May un
bless you!

Love—
Marla Aldridge-Hamrick

MW01593078

FROM CAPTIVE TO CAPTAIN

By
Karla Aldridge Hamrick

i

FROM CAPTIVE TO CAPTAIN

By
Karla Aldridge Hamrick

Copyright © 2004 Karla Aldridge Hamrick

ISBN 0-9754957-0-4

1st Printing – April 2004
Ballinger Printing & Graphics
Ballinger, Texas

ABOUT THE AUTHOR

Karla Rajean Aldridge was born on August 22, 1972 in San Angelo, Texas. At that time, her parents, Ray and Leta Aldridge lived in Jal, New Mexico, where her father worked for El Paso Natural Gas. The next year, he was transferred to Denver City, Texas. In 1976, the family moved to Robert Lee, Texas and Ray began working for Ivey Motor Company, a Ford dealership. Her mother began keeping children in her home. Karla and her sister, Kristi were the couple's only children until 1986. At that time, one of their cousins, William Aldridge, came to live with them, and the girls gained a brother. Ray still works for Ivey Motor Company and pastors Emmanuel Pentecostal Church. Leta keeps the church books, assists her aging parents, and works as a representative for Taihaitoan Noni, Inc.

In 1990, while Karla was a Senior in high school, she met the love of her life, Brian Lane Hamrick, at a speech tournament in Colorado City, Texas. He had been raised on a cotton farm by his parents, Bobby and Darlene Hamrick. His father also worked for the United States Postal Service as a rural mail carrier and raised Longhorn cattle. His mother worked for the

Loraine Senior Citizens. Brian later obtained a degree in Paramedicine from Texas State Technical Institute in Sweetwater, Texas. Karla holds a diploma from Angelo State University with a General Studies major, with concentrations in English, Government, and Psychology. Brian now works as Manager/Operator for Coke County Water Supply Corporation. The couple married in 1993 and have two daughters, Hanna Elise, eight years old, and Hunter Leiann, six years old. They are raising their girls in a house Karla's grandfather, James William Brantly Robertson, helped to build in the 1960s.

During her childhood years, much of Karla's free time was spent with her grandparents. In the summers, she would visit her father's parents in Jal, New Mexico and Kermit, Texas where her PaPa worked for El Paso Natural Gas. While at home in Robert Lee, she never missed an opportunity to visit the farm with her other grandfather, her Poppa. Her grandmother, Samantha Robertson, is known all over the county for her kindness, generosity, and cooking abilities. Both grandmothers doted on their grandchildren. Karla's large tight-knit family and her wonderful husband and children gave her the strength to write the novel while having to work full-time and directing Power Hour Children's Church. Her family and friends are very valuable to her, as is her faith. Coke County runs deep with Blair and Robertson blood, giving Karla a rich legacy.

ACKNOWLEDGMENTS

The following people deserve credit:

My husband, Brian Hamrick, for his love and support, reenacting a brave, and graphics design

My children, Hanna and Hunter, for doing all the extra chores and reenacting Ruby and Rebecca (The extra hugs and kisses did not hurt, either.)

My parents, Ray and Leta Aldridge, for lifelong love and support

My mother-in-law, Darlene Hamrick, for so much encouragement

My grandparents, Warren and Marion Aldridge and J.B. and Samantha Robertson, for all your love

My sister, Kristi Aldridge, reenacting Arizona Cain

My nephews, Jaden and Casey, reenacting school children

My aunt, Peggy Robertson, for proofreading and encouraging me

The rest of my family who supported me

Garland and Lana Richards, for research assistance

Annie Gill and Chase, reenacting and a great deal of help

Linda Burns, proofreader, friend and my first grade teacher

Kay Gothard, wonderful friend and supporter

Trish Ballew, proofreader, friend, and my junior high English teacher

Cindy Bessent, proofreader and friend

Dorothea Wright, proofreader, friend, and my high school Science teacher

Bobbie Allen, advertising, costume donations and a precious friend

Clay Allen , reenacting Red Horse and a lifelong friend

Sterling Myers, reenacting Samantha and a friend

Pat Percifull, reenacting a brave and a longtime friend

Abigayle Shelburne, reenacting school girl

The Fort Chadbourne Cavalry and wives, reenactors

 Paul Michalewicz and his history classes, for that last minute encouragement and show of support

Donna Poehls, costume donation and a dear friend

Sug Lawhon, costume donation and a special friend

Lane Jackson and Jesse Flores, Veribest ISD

LaQueta Shelburne, dear friend and supporter

Hal Spain and Melinda McCutchen, Observer/Enterprise

Karen De Los Santos, for assisting in numerous ways and being a great friend

Michael White, Ballinger Printing, for going the extra mile to help me

Angelo State University, Costume Director, Eldra Sanford

INTRODUCTION

Dear Reader,

One of my high school History teachers used to say, "We study events of the past in order to more clearly see and understand the future." Coach Edward Poehls branded these words into the permanent parts of our memories. While preparing this novel, I phoned him and asked if I could quote him. His exact response was something like this, "Why sure, you know that's basically the definition of history, don't you?" Then he paused and added, "You mean you wrote a book? When's your first signing? I want to be there." He, along with my husband, parents, and the rest of my family and friends encouraged me to follow my dream and gave me the strength and help I needed. I knew that God had given me abilities for a reason and perhaps I have discovered part of that calling.

Although I hope my work of fiction will be enjoyable to read, I also have a desire to show a different side of the "wild, wild west." Coke County was not founded on a bunch of drunk cowboys and wild Indians. There were many men and women of valor and strength, which dedicated their lives to bringing Christianity and civilization to the area. There were also Native Americans who worked and cooperated with the "white man" to develop the land on which I now reside. Over a period of years, the Comanche and other Indian tribes contributed fantastic knowledge of the region to aid the white man in realizing his American dream. For example, snakeweed has been used throughout the years and given to both animals and humans, suffering from rattlesnake bites.

As I was planning the photo shoot, I began looking for those who could play the parts of the Comanche warriors and chief. I had no difficulty finding prominent cheekbones. The Comanche were not all forced onto reservations. Many of them stayed and blended into the countryside. Others married the Anglos, and the results of such unions are still evident in our current residents.

There were times when the fear of the Comanche was so great that the windows would be boarded to prevent invasion.

Then, there are recordings of a great deal of interaction between the Native Americans and the Anglos. The following novel is my version of what might have happened when the times were somewhat peaceful between the fort and a particular tribe. While the tale is fiction, I have blended facts with my imaginations and based many of the stories on true happenings.

Finally, I must give credit to my great-uncle, Jefferson Davis Blair. He is now deceased, but was one of my favorite people when I was a child. I used to ride my bike to his house and thoroughly enjoyed his recounting of the past. My grandmother, Samantha Anna Mae Blair Robertson, added her knowledge to give me more information. Her faith in God has been passed to her children and then to me. Without Him, I would be nothing.

My sincere hope is that you will enjoy reading this book and gain strength and encouragement from it. This work was definitely a unified effort of family and friends.

Karla Rajean Aldridge-Hamrick

Figure 3. The Texas military frontier, 1852-1854. Figure reproduced from Smith 1999:7.

Dedication

This book is dedicated to my entire family and in memory of my deceased father-in-law, Bobby Gene Hamrick.

CHAPTER ONE

Ft. Chadbourne – July 1854

In one swift movement, she closed the gap between her and her prey. Rebecca Jane Blair had been chasing the same frog all the way from the fort to the creek. She had first spotted him hopping behind the mail station where she had been playing while the adults labored clearing the area after the hailstorm. They had all been so busy making repairs that they failed to notice the absence of the little girl. Rebecca decided from the moment she spotted the creature that she needed him for a pet. Her pursuit became so intense that she was standing two inches deep in the water of Oak Creek before she finally caught her quarry.

She climbed to the top of the embankment, found a large flat rock, and sat to acquaint herself with her newly found friend. The frog protested his capture and tried to wiggle free. Rebecca eased onto her back and crossed her legs, forgetting that little ladies were supposed to sit properly. The eight-year old bundle of energy squinted at the big West Texas sky, wondering if another storm was on its way. A hot breeze stirred the air as the unkind sun burned its path across the vastness of the untamed land.

"Now, now you's jus' calm yoself. Mamie Rebecca will take good care o' you." She crooned to the animal in a tone mocking her Mamie Eliza. The elderly Negro lady had been a part of the Blair family for two generations, exerting much influence over the children, especially for a slave woman. She had finished raising Rebecca's Pa,

Gemes, when his mother died during his young childhood.

As Rebecca continued to stroke the top of the frog's head and reassure him, she tried to decide what he was thinking. Did he have a Ma and Pa? Was he afraid of her? What kind of games did frogs like to play? Maybe he played "hop across the creek" with his friends like she did. She was so absorbed in her imaginings that she did not hear the distinctive rattle less than a foot from her head. Suddenly, the impact of an arrowhead hitting its target pierced the air, bringing Rebecca to an upright position. Fear held her motionless for a few seconds as she stared at the huge diamondback rattlesnake pinned to the hard Texas ground. As panic seized her chest, she realized that she had come close to either serious injury or death. The imminent threat of the rattlesnake was one lesson children were taught early and often.

Out of the corner of her eye, a movement brought Rebecca out of her shocked state. There, in a crouched position at the base of a large Oak tree, was the sternest looking Indian she had ever seen. He was not in the traditional dress worn to the council meetings, over which her Pa was usually in charge. Instead, he wore a red shirt and light blue boots, which the Comanche had come to favor and often requested in trades with the white man. A breastplate, made of coffee-stained bones, decorated the front of his shirt. He made no sound and sat so still he could have been a statue.

Red Horse gave no indication that a life or death moment had just passed. He had come to the creek to bathe and contemplate the next series of meetings he would be attending at Fort Chadbourne. As he neared the water's edge, he had noticed the child on the other side. She appeared to be holding a small animal and communicating with it. Her bonnet had fallen to her shoulders, exposing sandy-blond hair escaping the braids and ribbons. The bottom of her dress was saturated, and he suspected she had made her capture in the creek. The recent storm had blessed the area with much needed moisture, and the creek hummed a happy tune as the water gurgled over the rocks. However, a humid heat had followed, making the land seem more unbearable. He had not had long to observe her before her safety had been threatened. Nature took control as the Comanche reacted on instinct.

As the two strangers sat examining each other, Rebecca suddenly and swiftly skipped across the big rocks in the shallow part of the water, forgetting Mamie Eliza's warnings to take better care of her clothes. The red warrior was so stunned by the child's approach that he failed to react as her arms circled his neck in gratitude, almost knocking him to the ground. She was back on her side of the creek, running toward the officers' quarters, before he had time to respond. Then, the realization of her actions hit him full force as the intenseness of her green eyes pierced his memory. He had seen identical, deep, reflective pools of fire somewhere in his past. Who was she? Something about her unusual courage stirred him. Most of the white children he had observed did not have the courage to approach a warrior, especially one they had not ever seen. She had expressed her gratitude bravely and without hesitation.

Red Horse remained crouched and still, listening to the river and reflecting on the day until the sun began to descend behind the low, rolling hills. As he rose to return to the campsite, a strange thought suddenly occurred

3

to him. Those unusual eyes and brave spirit seemed inevitably linked to a little boy from his youth. As he made his way across the grassy plain, his thoughts were focused on a raid made on white settlers when he was a young brave. The capture of the young boy with fiery green eyes had remained a legend among his people. The mysterious escape of the child had spooked the superstitious nature of the Comanche people. Many tales had spread from the event and been told in the native Uto-Aztecan language.

Rebecca raced to the south side of the fort and bounded up the steps, throwing her arms around Mamie Eliza's waist. "Chil' where has you been? I'z been sick with worry and yo' ma be thinkin' all'z kinds o' bad thoughts."

"I'm sorry Mamie, but look what I found. Isn't he adorable?" She held the frog high for inspection making an innocent face while Eliza tried to hide her amusement.

"Chil' you be knowin' yo ma ain't gonna have the likes o' that creature in her house." Eliza confirmed Rebecca's doubts about her Ma's probable disapproval.

"Please, talk to her Mamie, pleeeease!" Rebecca pleaded with such desperation that her Mamie could not help but take pity on her.

"Now, now you be knowin' tha's out o' the question, but I has a plan. You give me yo' new frien' an' I's take him to my home an' you can come see him any time you want."Eliza had a bad habit of spoiling her youngest charge.

"Oh, thank you Mamie and I promise I'll take care of him every day." Rebecca was already inside the house, assigned to the Captain and his family, before her Mamie had time to respond, much less change her mind.

The officer's quarters were made of large, flat rock which was native to the area and much easier to find than lumber. The nearest city to obtain such supplies was San Antonio; so, the fort had to depend on many natural resources.

Eliza proceeded down the front steps of the rock house and made her way to the servants' quarters with her skirt gently blowing in the afternoon breeze. She was so thankful, especially today, that the accepted culture of the west allowed women to desert their petticoats, due to the extreme heat. She quickened her pace as she realized suppertime was fast approaching. She was glad now that she had spent the day before making bread, as this morning she had felt obligated to assist with the repair efforts. The aftermath of the storm had seemed impossibly devastating with roofs strewn all over the grounds and debris littering the tall grasses. Yet, due to the unified efforts of the soldiers and residents of the fort, the area was beginning to look livable again. She had not ever seen such unity among a large group of people as when Captain Gemes Blair was in charge. She took a special pride in his accomplishments knowing she had helped mold the character of this complex, yet strong man.

The inside of her quarters, which she shared with two other female servants, were sparsely furnished, but Gemes had made sure that the necessary repairs were made quickly, earning him the gratitude of those who served him. Eliza deposited the small creature in the coffee can she had used the last time Rebecca had captured a pet. She shook her head and looked at the ceiling, talking to God as she so often did when she was alone. "Lord, you be knowin' I done raised my share of these Blair chillens, but I done be thinkin' I's got my han's full this time."

Eliza was pouring the hot, rice soup into the serving bowl when Samantha opened the door and asked her if she needed any help. Although custom did not call for the wife to assist the servants, things had always been different with the Blair family. A combination of Biblical teachings on God's love for all humanity and tragic circumstances had created a unique relationship between servant and owner. "Now 'Missus Mantha you's know that I don' 'spect yo help, mo' specially since you's been slavin' so hard to be helpin' Mistuh Gemes"

"Now Mamie, you and I both know that you have worked as hard as anyone today" Samantha tried to hide her concern for her aging friend. She owed so much of her happiness to this kind-hearted lady, knowing that she was largely responsible for Gemes becoming the man he had. She often prayed that the Lord would keep her in the best of health for many more years, or at least until Rebecca was grown. That child took the energy of three people.

Samantha Jane Blair had been born in a small community in Tennessee to Mary and Brantly Robertson. Her parents had owned a large plantation and had hoped their youngest daughter would marry well. Gemes was not from a poor family, but he was not necessarily wealthy either. However, his incredible ability to deal with people and his common sense had quickly earned the respect of Samantha's Pa. She could still remember the look of admiration on her Pa's face the first time Gemes had solved a business dilemma for him. Her mind was so far in the past that she almost dropped the bowl of soup when the

6

door swung open, startling her.

"Ma, can I invite someone to dinner tomorrow night?" Rebecca asked in the most polite tone she could muster and looking as angelic as possible.

"May I, Rebecca, and what in this world have you done to your clothes?" Samantha shook her head in despair. She did not understand why a pretty, little girl wanted to traipse all over the place and act like a boy.

"I'm sorry Ma. I accidentally stepped in the creek while I was chasing a frog." At least Rebecca usually told the truth, even if it meant serious consequences. She stared at a spot on the floor, fidgeting with her dress and waiting on her mother's reaction.

"Rebecca Jane! I ought to switch you good. You go change your clothes and then find your seat at the table. Tomorrow, you will wash and repair your dress instead of Mamie. Do you hear me?" Her blue eyes held a look that told her daughter she had better walk softly for a few days. Rebecca quickly left to do as she was told while Mamie and Ma made their way from the kitchen to the main house with the food.

"Dear Lord, I pray that you would help us today to do your will and follow your leading. I ask you for special favor tomorrow as I hold council with the natives of this land. I pray, Dear Father, that you not let us forget that you made all men equal and that you died for all of mankind. And Lord, if you don't see fit to give us this land as our own, then help us be wise enough to leave it to the Comanche. We thank you for your blessings and this food. Amen." Gemes ended the prayer and lifted a spoon of soup to his mouth. Before he could take a bite, Rebecca sprang from her chair and raced to the front door.

"I hear him, Pa! I really do! He's finally back. Maybe he will tell us some stories while we eat and teach me to shoot his gun tomorrow!" Rebecca threw open the door to admit her favorite uncle, Jefferson Davis Blair. His scouting job had prevented any romance in his life so he spent his free time doting on Gemes' and Samantha's children, especially his little Bec. He scooped her into his arms as she squealed with delight. Her older sister, Ruby stood in the background, like a perfect little lady. She bore a much closer resemblance to the Robertson family, while Rebecca was unmistakably her father's blood.

"Hello, Uncle Jeff." Ruby stepped forward and gently hugged him. She had her mother's grace, beauty, and gentle manner. She enjoyed learning how to sew and she often helped Mamie and her Ma make clothes for the rest of the family.

"Jeff, I am so glad you have once more returned safely to us." Samantha breathed a sigh of relief as her brother-in-law lightly kissed her cheek. She enjoyed his time with them for many reasons, but was most grateful for the bond between brothers that seemed to conquer any difficulty.

The brothers exchanged a warm, firm handshake as the rest of the family returned to the table. "Jeff, we have a lot to discuss, but let's fill our boots first." They both chuckled at Mamie's old joke about where they managed to put all the food they ate. As they were making their way to the table, the source of their humor entered the room.

"Oh, Lord, You be knowin' I can't handle any mo' o' these Blairs!" Eliza called to the ceiling while the room erupted in laughter.

"Mamie, one of these days somebody's going to think

you really hate me." Jeff chuckled as he grabbed her in a bear hug. She was the closest thing to a mother he had ever known. Gemes had vague memories of their ma before she died giving birth to his younger brother, but Jeff had only been left with a few photos. He now fought tears as he realized how much Eliza was beginning to age.

"Tell us a story, pleeease!" Rebecca emphasized the last word hoping to be granted her request.

"Rebecca Jane Blair, where are your manners? You know children are not to control the conversation at the table." Samantha's voice was stern, yet gentle as she secretly hoped for the same thing as her daughter.

"Let him eat first and then if he wants, he may tell us a story," Gemes knew his brother must be tired and hungry from his long journey. Scouting was not only dangerous, but lonely and exhausting. Many times the scout would go days with nothing to eat but a few pieces of dried beef and strong, bitter coffee to drink.

Rebecca spent the rest of the meal in silence, while the adults exchanged talk of the recent storm. She just wished they would all be quiet and let her Uncle Jeff tell her about the Indians he had met. He never failed to have a wild tale to share. Her pa insisted that sometimes the stories were concocted merely to entertain his youngest daughter, but Rebecca just knew they must be true.

"Gemes, are all the roofs sufficiently repaired, or could you use another pair of hands for a few days." Jeff had obtained orders to stay at the fort until he was told differently

Gemes scooted his chair back from the table and stretched his long, aching legs. "We have managed to provide some sort of covering for all the barracks, but the entire fort is far from being completely repaired. I wired San Antonio today asking for assistance with materials, but who knows how long that will take. For now, we will use what we can scrounge up and make do with what we have. I can always use another set of hard-working hands. You know that."

"Now, Gemes don't work him so hard he never comes back. I need him around to keep you in line." Samantha enjoyed teasing her husband and delighted in his apparent closeness with his little brother. The happiness they shared provided much needed relief from the stress of the day to day harshness of life at the fort. The fact that they had not had a single potato for over six months was even forgotten the minute Jeff had entered the room.

"Well, I reckon I'd better work hard at telling a story, or Rebecca will die of boredom." He laughed in his own unique way in which the sound seemed to roll from the bottom of his belly, his head tilting back to add to the volume. Rebecca rushed to sit beside his chair while Ruby and the adults merely leaned forward in anticipation.

THE INDIAN THIEF

One night I had made camp somewhere north of here after a quiet day and no sign of the Comanche. I had built a small fire, hoping that the smoke would not be seen from very far. I had one piece of hard, dry jerky left and just enough coffee for one last pot. I put the coffee on the fire to brew and decided to make my way to a nearby creek and wash off some of the grime from riding. I hadn't had a bath in a week. My canteen was might near empty too and needed filling. I had draped my shirt and britches on a low limb of an oak tree while I was bathing. The water felt good and I drank my fill before filling my canteen. I had just begun to relax and unwind when I heard a rustle in the trees. At first, I thought it was just the wind, and then, I watched my britches disappear from the tree. Before I had time to say, "Scat!" a young slip of an Indian ran up the bank of that creek and disappeared. I ran as fast as I could, but you and I both know that no white man can ever catch a Comanche. So, there I was with a shirt and no britches. Well, I thought about making me a skirt of leaves like Adam and Eve, but wasn't real sure how to go about it. Well, I figured I had already made camp for the night, so I ate my meager supper, dampened the fire with water from the creek, and then crawled into my bedroll.

Sometime during the night, another strange sound made me sit up straight with the hairs on the back of my neck standing at attention. In a minute, a strange looking cowboy sauntered up to my bedroll. He only had two teeth in his whole head and smelled like he had spent a year on the trail. He introduced himself as Tom Morris from San Antonio. He said he had been looking for some land to claim and figured that he had best explore without his family first. Well, let me tell you, I decided I should have taken my chances and ridden without britches all night long instead of spending the night with the likes of him.

The next morning he loaned me an extra set of britches he had in his roll. Then, he followed me to the next town and waited for me to buy some more. I'm sure those folks smelled us for miles before we got there too. I'm pretty sure we stunk worse than an old dead cow. Now Bec, the next time you see an Indian with a pair of scout britches on, you look real close. They just might be mine.

Gemes was shaking his head in dismay while everyone else's laughter shook the room. How Jeff could come up with such nonsense was beyond his brother's understanding, but he certainly was entertaining. Scouts did not even really have a set uniform; so, just what were scout pants supposed to look like anyway? Gemes had decided in the last few months that he needed to work real hard at finding himself a sister-in-law. He knew his wife would enjoy the company, and Jeff sure could use some supervision. Though, the Lord only knew, where he would find anyone out in this wild country. The way Rebecca was at scheming maybe he should let her in on his thoughts, but that would certainly be flirting with disaster.

The men rose from the table and made their way outside onto the porch while the women began to clear the food and dishes. Rebecca began to inwardly fume about being a girl and not getting to wear britches and go outside with the men after meals. She especially hated having to sit still for lessons and during Bible readings on Sundays. Right now, she hurried to finish her chores just in case her uncle felt like telling some more stories before bedtime.

The twenty-two year old scout scooted the stump to the front of the porch and perched on it like he did not have a care in the world. His brother chose to lean on the wood railing. Both men were tall and muscular, but the similarities ended there. Jeff tended to scorch in the hot sun while Gemes turned darker every day. Jeff's blue eyes had been a gift from their father, and their mother had passed her unique, green emeralds to Gemes. Jeff removed his hat and ran his hand through his blond hair. How often he had wondered if his mother's hair had been the same as Gemes, dark blond with a hint of red, glistening under the sun.

Both men had Eliza to thank for their determined spirits. Self-pity had not been tolerated by her, and she always found something good in every situation. The day they had lost their father, she had grieved briefly and then held her head high, determined she must be strong for her boys. The color of their skin had made them no less hers, and she had done her best to honor their mother's values and beliefs in raising them. From the few pearls of knowledge Jeff had gained about his mother, he surmised she had been quite a lady. He suspected his father had never remarried, because no one could take her place in his heart. Plus, he had Eliza to love and nurture his children.

"I met Red Horse about five miles out of the fort on my way in today." Jeff began to relay the information to the captain. "He had on the shirt he got at the last council. Maybe red shirts are gonna be more valuable than guns after all." He chuckled as he removed the pipe from his pocket.

"I bet the Comanche have had to make more pipes too. Looks like somebody sure enjoys getting those in trade." Gemes was forever harassing Jeff about scaring all the women away with his tobacco. He also liked to tease him about joining the Indians when they smoked their ceremonial peace pipe.

"You're just jealous 'cause you know Samantha will come after you with a shotgun if she catches you with a pipe in your mouth." Jeff's laugh brought his niece scurrying onto the porch.

"Ya tellin' stories again, Uncle Jeff?" She had heard him laughing and just knew he could not possible be discussing serious things like peace talks.

"Rebecca, you know that your uncle and I have to take care of some business. He just can't be serious 'bout much of anything." Gemes mildly chastised his daughter sending her disappointed back into the house.

"I'm seriously glad that you have to raise that young 'un and not me." Jeff roared again, this time reaching up to give his brother a light punch on the arm.

"Did Red Horse mention tomorrow's council?" As much as he enjoyed the camaraderie, the captain had to collect his thoughts and focus on the upcoming meeting.

"Just briefly. He seemed really preoccupied with something. Maybe, they're planning some kind of raid on us and using these peace talks as a front." Jeff expressed his concern, hoping he was wrong.

Gemes turned to face him and shook his head. "No, there was a time when I would have thought the same thing, but Red Horse has done wonders with his band. Somehow, he has gained their respect without using scalps to do it. They seem to listen to him. We just have to do the honorable thing and not try to trick them."

"What if you receive orders to do differently?" The younger man knew that so often the choices the fort leaders had to make were based on orders from Washington and had little to do with their own judgements.

"The politicians figured out a long time ago I don't base my dealings on lies. When they give me my walking papers I'll be glad to leave, but until then I intend to keep on doing things my way." He had no intention of going

14

back on his word to anybody, even a Comanche. However,he still shuddered anytime he heard a sound resembling anything close to their war cries. His memory would then take him back to the day he truly had become a man.

"You still think about it don't ya?" Jeff could read his thoughts and knew that the ghost of the past still haunted him. The only reason the Captain had been able to cope as well as he had was because of a talk he and Eliza had had one night when he was thirteen.

"I reckon I try not to. Not much use in dwelling on things that can't be changed. Anyway hanging onto the past only hinders the future." Gemes referred to one of Mamie's favorite sayings. "I do know that the Comanche aren't to be fooled with, and if we ever think we want any of this land, we had better keep our word."

"I saw a band of Kiowas near Fort Worth, but they were headed north and I don't expect them to be of any concern to you here." Jeff changed the subject back to the business at hand. "Maybe Fort Chadbourne can be an example to the rest of them and show them how to really handle things."

"Yeah, but you know the politicians. They don't even live in the real world. Money, land, power–now those are the things they understand." Gemes had his doubts that Washington would ever learn from their mistakes. It seemed like after enough massacres they would learn to leave well enough alone.

The front door opened and Eliza stepped onto the porch, still amused by her bedtime conversation with Rebecca. She had wanted to know if her mother would be upset if she invited an Indian warrior to supper. Eliza wondered what Rebecca had been doing all day that had put such notions in her head. Sometimes, ignorance was bliss where that child was concerned. Rebecca had seemed determined to find a way to convince her mother to allow her to extend the invitation despite her Mamie's warnings that the subject should probably not ever be mentioned.

Although Eliza had come so far in her ability to forgive, sometimes the very thought of losing any of the family she had grown to love was unbearable. She could not help the fear that swelled in her throat when she remembered the fateful day of bloodshed that had almost taken Gemes from them forever. There would always be some misgivings inside of her when she faced a Comanche, no matter how hard she tried to let go of the past. She suspected that Samantha's doubts about the Indians came from similar fears. Gemes seemed to have let go of the bad memories better than anyone, and he tried to do right by the Comanche to the best of his ability.

"I wonder what Rebecca was up to today." Eliza heard the captain's voice as she made her way to her hut. "I have a funny feeling that the frog she found was the least of her adventures."

"What makes you say that?" Jeff quizzed his brother with a hint of amusement in his voice. "I know, she's just like you; so, you can read her like a book."

"More like, she's just like you and I done been there and done that!" Gemes attempted to push his brother off of the stump as he headed back into the house. Jeff rose and followed him, laughing at the return jibe.

Jeff stretched his tall frame onto the cot his sister-in-law had prepared him in the front room. He was thinking how much better it felt to be inside instead of on the hard ground, battling the elements when Rebecca tiptoed into the room. "Are you asleep Uncle Jeff?'

"Not yet Bec, what's up?" He smiled in the dark knowing that she delighted in his stories and soaked up all the attention he gave her. If he could find a woman that loved him like his Bec did, then he might just have to settle down and get married.

"Could you tell me just one more story please?" Rebecca appealed to her uncle's gentle heart by leaning over and kissing his forehead.

"If I do, then will you promise to go right to bed and not give your Ma or your Mamie any trouble tomorrow." He decided to make up for all his teasing and do something nice for Samantha. So, he used the opportunity to bribe his niece with a story in exchange for good behavior.

"Yes Sir, I won't have time to do anything else anyway, because I have to mend my dress tomorrow instead of Mamie. Ma said!" She tried to make her uncle feel sorry for her with her disheartened tone and expression, but all she got from him was another one of his deepthroated chuckles.

"Has your Pa told you that he was captured by the Comanche when he wasn't much older than you?" He had been reluctant to share the truth with his niece but maybe, it was time she understood her Pa a little better.

"Tell me Uncle Jeff, tell me!" Her green eyes danced with delight, matching the blue sparkle in Jeff's eyes as he sat up and prepared to thrill his niece.

GEME'S CAPTURE

I was just a little guy; so, I don't remember much of what was going on. But I do remember, we had left Tennessee to come to Texas and, we were all tired of being on the trail. I guess everybody had pretty much let their guard down and decided that the Indians were going to leave us alone when everything changed. We heard the loudest whooping and hollering you can imagine, louder than the worst Texas thunderstorm. The Comanche swooped down on us like a bunch of hawks with their machetes raised ready to devour the whole lot of us. They killed most of the men and took several of our women and children. They tried to kill your Pa, but he fought bravely, killing the first two Indians that got near him with his rifle. Well, the Comanche decided that he was courageous and would make an excellent brave; so, they captured him instead of killing him. I would have loved to have seen them take him back to their camp; I suspect your Pa made them wish they'd of killed him. They tied him to a stump 'til they could decide which family should have him. He kept fighting and kept trying to get loose.

Meanwhile, what was left of our wagon train was in mourning. We made camp for the night, and Mamie started praying. Men from another wagon train that had crossed our path later that day joined the men that were left. They began to organize a search party and bury the dead. Long after the simple burials, Mamie was still begging the Lord for mercy. The next morning we awoke to a strange sound coming from outside our camp. The men grabbed the few rifles the Comanche had overlooked and prepared to fight, deciding the Indians had returned to finish what they had started. Mamie stopped them saying, "No, No, it's Gemes. I jus' knows it! The Lord promised me last night that he would give us our boy back!" Well, sure enough it was your Pa with his hands still tied behind his back and his feet still bound together. Between his feisty attitude and Mamie's angels, he had managed to work himself free of that stump and hop his way to freedom. We had ourselves a celebration and Mamie liked to have never stopped hugging her little Mastuh! I decided right then that I never wanted to be on Mamie's bad side, cause that would make me an enemy of the angels too. I also figured your Pa wasn't one to mess with if he could outsmart the Comanche.

Rebecca lay in bed that night thinking of her uncle's story and his warnings not to ever discuss it with her Pa unless he mentioned it first. She could tell by his seriousness that her uncle was not just creating a wild tale. Somehow, she knew that this time he was for sure telling her a truth from her Pa's childhood. So, why was her Pa so bent on helping the Comanche? She had heard Mamie talk so often about the need to forgive. Was this Pa's way of forgiving? Even if it was, why was he so secretive about his past? She fell asleep with more questions in her mind that she was determined to ask Mamie tomorrow. She hoped someday she would understand her Pa.

CHAPTER TWO

PEACE TALKS

Long before the red sun peaked over the hills, Gemes had been making his way around the fort preparing for the day. First, he had coffee with all the officers and decided who would attend council with him. Then, he posted extra soldiers around the fort to increase security. Although there had been no skirmishes since he had taken command at Fort Chadbourne, he still felt a need to be alert. He made his way back to his quarters just as the hundreds of Indians began to swarm into the fort. The warriors kept a tight vigil during the meetings, but only the chiefs were allowed to actually attend the council.

As she prepared the morning meal, Eliza whistled a hymn and occasionally offered a prayer for the day's business. Her joints were aching, and she decided that another storm must be on its way. One of the blessings of old age was that her body could forecast the weather. She secretly was hoping the trades today would result in some fresh meat. The soldiers stayed so busy that there was little time left for hunting. She poured the gravy into a bowl and prepared to serve her family. As she glanced out the kitchen window, she watched the numerous Indian camps in the distance and knew that soon the fort would be crawling with activity.

"Mornin' Eliza," Gemes addressed his servant with the same respect he would any lady.

"I expect we'll have another hot, humid day; so, I don't want you working too hard." He couldn't help being concerned about what the severity of their living conditions was doing to all of them. Sometimes, the constant need for rain became overwhelming, let alone the daily threats that faced them. He had decided that the rattlesnake was a much more precarious enemy than the Comanche would ever be, especially since Chief Yellow Wolf had decided to raid South Texas and leave them alone for the time being.

"Mistuh Gemes, you's the one that be needin' prayer now. You's got a heavy load on them shouldu's." She bestowed a motherly look of love on him and proceeded to the main house with the rest of the food. The other members of the family joined them, and the meal began.

Rebecca appeared unusually fidgety over breakfast and hurried to help clear the table. She quickly took her dress outside to the washtub, full of water from the creek. Using a bar of lye soap, she scrubbed the red mud from the cloth, wishing she could be finished and go check on her frog. Besides, she was hoping to get a closer look at the visitors.

Ruby watched her younger sister from the window as she was washing the breakfast dishes. She had told her to go on and clean her dress, and they would dry the plates together when she was done. Ruby could not help but take pity on Rebecca at times. She did not intend to get into so much trouble; it just seemed to find her. Ruby knew that Bec had a good heart and did her best to do what was right. Some girls just were not cut out to be little angels. While Ruby enjoyed feminine activities, Rebecca was much happier exploring. Rebecca finished the job and made her way to the kitchen to help her older sister. Even though they had servants, their Ma and Pa believed all children should learn responsibility; so, many of the smaller chores were theirs to do.

"Ruby, do you think the Comanche still like blond scalps." Rebecca had no qualms about asking gruesome questions. Sometimes, when she was alone with her only doll or at the creek with one of her pets, she would imagine that she was the first female Indian warrior and that her life was full of exciting events.

"Rebecca, why on earth would you say a thing like that?" Ruby was appalled at her little sister's line of questioning. She especially did not like her thinking of such things when the Indians were all over the fort, and she was already more than apprehensive.

"Dunno, anyway we don't have to worry. Both of us have Pa's dirty blond hair anyway, and we're not real white either. Maybe they'll think we're part Injun and leave us alone." Rebecca pronounced her conclusion proudly and with confidence tilting her head up in a defiant manner.

"Bec that's silly. Ma's part Dutch and Pa's Irish; so, I seriously doubt anyone will think we have red blood in us." The older sister referred to the slang term used often by the soldiers.

"Better not let Mamie hear you talk like that. She gets pretty upset when we talk about people as a color." She delighted in chastising Ruby; the roles were usually reversed. She folded the towel and placed it on the board, which had been mounted to the wall. Countertops were a luxury not afforded the kitchen; so, rough boards took their places.

Ruby pinned Rebecca's dress over the open window to dry, hoping the wind would blow through it and cool the inside of the building. Then, the air would not be so stifling while they prepared lunch.

Rebecca ran as fast as her legs could take her to the servants' quarters to retrieve her frog. She had decided on a name for him and couldn't wait to see if he approved. She thought about trying to make war paint to put on his face. Then, she would have her very own brave. Maybe together, they could start their own tribe. She continued concocting various plans in her mind as she raced back to the other side of the fort.

"Greetings Chief Red Horse." The sound of her Pa's voice stopped Rebecca in her tracks. She quickly stepped behind the building with her pet held tightly in her hand. She wanted to see what the chief looked like, so she edged closer to the house. Her mother had always insisted they stay far away from the council meetings. The feelings were mutual to both cultures, as the Comanche did not allow their women to speak to white men.

Rebecca thought she would faint when she realized her Pa was talking to her rescuer, and he still had on the same shirt he had worn the day before when she had encountered him at the creek. Either they did not wash their clothes very often or took real good care of them. He carried a buffalo hide and a peace pipe. Beside the steps, stood two stern looking braves. They had already presented the buffalo meat in trade and stood staunch still with no expression on their sun-parched faces. They wore the traditional Comanche dress which included head-dresses made of buffalo horns and necklaces decorated with beads and bear claws. Their leather leggings were trimmed with long fringes and their faces displayed bright stripes of paint. A streak of lightning bolted across the sky as Rebecca watched the men continue into the house.

The light tapping on her shoulder caused Rebecca to spin around quickly. She stifled a scream as a little, dark hand closed over her mouth to prevent the sound from escaping. He put his finger to his mouth in a gesture asking her to stay quiet. He gave her a minute to compose herself and then slowly lowered his hand.

The two stood inspecting each other for several moments. Rebecca had only seen Comanche children at a distance; now, she was getting a real close look at two big, brown eyes. The little brave wore his hair loosely draped around his shoulders with a wide band, keeping it out of his eyes. He tried to scowl like his father did when wanting to intimidate someone, but his steady gaze was met with fire. He had met his match.

Little Running Water squatted beside the officer's quarters and motioned for Rebecca to join him. He was just as curious about these meetings as she was and had been biding his time for the right chance to eavesdrop. His father had learned a limited amount of the white man's vocabulary and had been teaching what he knew to his son. Likewise, Rebecca's Pa had acquired an understanding of a few of the Comanche terms. At night, when he relaxed on the front porch, he would often teach Rebecca some of the new language.

Their first encounter involved a lot of listening and little talking. During the first hour, Rebecca and Little Running Water had managed to understand that the leaders in Washington wanted Captain Blair to convince Red Horse to relocate his tribe to a decent area of land on the Brazos River near Ft. Belknap. Captain Blair secretly felt that the politicians were simply edging the tribe closer to

Oklahoma but did not voice his concerns. Red Horse agreed to do some thinking on the matter, but had not committed to the move. Then, some trading had taken place, and the two children grew bored listening to their fathers' discussion.

Rebecca followed Little Running Water to the creek and stuck her toe in it, wishing she could go for a swim. Little Running Water stood on a rock, watching Rebecca swing her bonnet in her hands. The sun painted different colors in her hair while she suddenly remembered to tell her frog his new name, Benjamin Franklin. She had liked the stories of his experiments so much that Mr. Franklin had become one of her favorite heroes. As she talked to her pet, Little Running Water stood examining her. She seemed to be one with nature, just like he had always been taught to be. He decided she would fit well into his tribe. At eleven years old, he was beginning to think about his future. The life of a Comanche boy was tough at best. He was expected to endure incredible hardships to prove his manhood and the tests of his strength had already begun.

"Me see hop," Rebecca could not help giggling at Little Running Water's limited English. She extended her hand for him to take the frog. Just as she did, Benjamin Franklin saw his moment of opportunity and leaped from her palm. Before she had time to be sad, her new friend had sprung into action. Faster than a jackrabbit, he managed to catch the animal before he made his escape across the water. Before the children had a chance to enjoy their victory, the skies opened and the rain began to fall.

"Rebecca Jane Blair! Where are you? You must come at once!" Rebecca heard the urgent call from her mother and quickly waved to Little Running Water as she raced back to the fort.

"Here I am Ma. I was just taking a walk." She told part of the truth, anyway, to her worried parent. She stood on the porch and began to wring the water out of her dress under a disapproving frown. Rebecca's hair hung in soggy strips around her face. Her braids were half undone, and her shoes were muddy. In contrast, her mother stood before her, impeccably dressed with a starched apron covering the front of her skirt and her hat so stiff that the sides stood at attention.

"Rebecca, you know that I want you to stay close to the house when these meetings are taking place. I just don't feel safe with all these Comanche taking over the fort like they're about to scalp us all and leave with the loot." Samantha almost wished during peace talks that her husband was not the commanding officer. The councils took place in the front room of their home. The other officers with families lived in jackal huts behind the main row of living quarters. Their houses were crudely made buildings of limbs, brush, and mud. She was the only mother that could not totally isolate her children from the events of the day. At least, they would have fresh meat for supper.

The soldiers had boarded most of the windows inside the fort the night before the meeting. The fear of the Comanche was so great, especially among the women, that the residents stayed hidden from view during the day-long ordeal.

Long after the fort had been cleared of the Comanche men, Captain Blair felt restless. He had experienced too many unexpected happenings with the tribes to ever feel

27

completely at ease. After the evening meal, he had quickly retired to the porch, not feeling like answering his family's persistent questions. He knew he should be more reassuring with them, especially the children, but he did not want to give them false hope. He had felt better today, knowing that Jeff was by his side. The front door opened and his little brother joined him, lighting his new pipe from Red Horse.

Both men sat silently for a long time, listening to the falling rain and the sound of thunder. Jeff respected his brother's need for silence and just offered his quiet company. No one felt the pressure of the task at hand like the commanding officer. Gemes had not only his reputation in the army to uphold but felt a sense of loyalty to anyone he made a promise. When he gave a man his word, he did not ever go back on what he said. Sometimes his honesty caused him extra grief with the United States government.

"I think maybe we will find peace with this group of tribes if we can keep Yellow Wolf out of this part of the country," Gemes finally spoke, the lightning exposing the deep creases etched in his forehead.

"I reckon we haven't seen the last of him though the way he keeps raiding," Jeff had continued to hear stories of the legendary chief's tirades when he was on his last scouting mission. Many times, he had witnessed the aftermath of Yellow Wolf's cruel attacks.

"Maybe not, but he's gotta die sometime. No man is immortal and the more peace we can make, the less battles we'll have to fight," His deep voice echoed in the hot night air as he turned to look at his brother and trusted friend. His gleaming, green eyes shined in the dark, like a cat's.

"Gemes, do you remember the night we lost Pa?"

Jeff's question caught Gemes off guard since it seemed totally off the subject.

"Of course I remember. Why would you ask such a thing?" He answered gruffly. The day they buried his father had been the only time in his life that he had felt totally powerless. Losing his role model had taken the wind from his sails, and he had been forced to fight hard to rekindle his determination and zest for life.

"Well, Mamie and I had a long talk about immortality. She pointed out that Pa's body might be buried, but his legacy would never die. I don't know, but it seems like a point worth remembering." After his statement was made, Jeff stood and walked back in the house without ever looking back at his brother.

That same night, in the Indian camp, there was a huge celebration taking place. The Comanche did not need much of an excuse. Since this day had brought a portion of peace between them and the white men, they enjoyed their sun dance instead of the usual war dance. In one area of camp a foot race was taking place among the young boys. Little Running Water won as usual. While the party continued, he slipped into his tipi to check on the frog. The storm had prevented him from returning it to the little white girl. He had enjoyed the small amount of time he had spent with her and wished that life was different and would allow them to associate with each other. He knew, however, that the Comanche distrusted the white men as much as they were distrusted. Maybe someday, someday...

"Little Running Water, my son, you look so sad. What keeps my little spirit of life from enjoying the fun?" Red

Horse had sensed all afternoon that something was troubling his offspring. He had been waiting for a chance to approach him.

"Father, I don't like our world so much sometimes." The boy had been taught to be frank and direct, which was the Comanche way.

"I know, son, things were so much simpler before the white man came and brought diseases and took away so much of our land." Red Horse remembered a time when the American Indian was the chief of the land.

"No, Father, it wasn't. Even then, we fought with the Kiowa and the Sioux. There has always been fighting and wars. Why must there always be conflict of some kind? There is plenty of land. Why can't those who are different from us share the land and why can't we let them?" Little Running Water shook his head sadly.

"My son, as long as there has been life, there has been greed. I am working hard on our tribe and our leaders to make a better world for you and your children. I have hope, since they recently appointed me Civil Chief. Usually this position is reserved for an older man. There are many here many moons ahead of me; so, they must have a great deal of respect for me. I try hard to make a difference. Sometimes, peace comes at a high price though. Remember that!" He then turned and lifted the flap to open the tipi. Two young feet walked in his footsteps back to the excitement.

Later, that night, Red Horse sat on the bank of the creek, counting the cost of peace. He knew that the only way peace could come to the Comanche would be at the expense of their way of life. They would have to relinquish the freedom of their ways and their land. The white man would drive the buffalo to far away places, and the Comanche would starve or be at the mercy of others. He hoped that Captain Blair would make a better life for the Comanche, and make sure that the nation did not die. Red Horse suddenly felt overwhelmingly vulnerable, his future in the hands of a white man he hoped would not betray him.

Eliza entered Rebecca's room and leaned over the bed to kiss her good night. She always waited until Samantha had tucked in her daughters and then followed suit. She respected her Missus and knew her place in the home.

"Mamie, what does it mean to be free?" Rebecca's continuous curiosity had long since ceased to surprise Eliza.

"Well, I reckon that depends on who's askin'. Why?" She had a feeling they were about to discuss the issue of slavery again.

"Well, like now that we're in Texas, and you are called a servant instead of a slave, does that mean you're free?" Rebecca had never liked the idea of her Mamie being called a slave anymore than her Pa did. She was glad for the different code in the untamed West.

"Rebecca I's been free a long time now ya hear me? Oh, I s'pose I'd like the idea of not bein' owned an' all. I don' s'pose they's a body alive that wan's to be counted as a piece o' property, but I's got a wonderful family an' I's got my Lord. Tha's all a body really needs. Ya see, I's seen lots o' folks that u's slaves to many thin's like stron' drink an' money an' power. I guess I'm might near as free as mos'. Now you's go to sleep an' quit worryin' yo' pretty lil head with such thoughts. Ya hear me now?"

She leaned over the bed and placed a kiss on the child's cheek.

"Yes Mamie, but one more question. Do you still pray for God to free your family?" Rebecca's question stopped the elderly lady as she started out of the room. She had been unaware that the child had heard her nightly prayer. When had the child been able to listen outside of her window at night? Eliza felt panic at the thought of Rebecca exploring in the dark.

So many members of Eliza's family served cruel masters. At times, she almost felt guilty for the opportunities she had been afforded. Mister Gemes' Pa had not even allowed her to refer to him as her master. She stood with tears in her eyes remembering the day he had purchased her from the nightmare in which she had lived as a child. He had bought her just a week before her seventeenth birthday. Her life had changed drastically, and as long as she did not think about the family she never got the chance to see, then she was basically happy. Her peace of mind came from those she had grown to love.

As she left the room she responded, "Yes, Bec I's pray ever' night, ever' night–someday, someday." Her hope of someday lingered in the night air as she made her way across the grasses of the fort. For now, the white man lived in his stone house, the Negro servant lived in a jackal hut on the opposite side, and the Comanche made his home under the stars in a tipi by the creek.

CHAPTER THREE

PAYDAY

Ruby, can you keep a secret?" Rebecca had been dying to share her idea with someone for two days, but she had not had the opportunity. She and her sister were doing the breakfast dishes while their mother and Mamie made the beds. The sun was shining through the windows promising a hot day.

"Bec I seriously hope that you're not up to something that will get us both in trouble." She had learned to be a bit leery of Rebecca's plans. More than once, they had both been in trouble over her schemes.

"This is a wonderful idea, I promise!" She stated emphatically as she dried the last dish and hopped onto the rough board.

"Bec, get down from there! You'll pull it out of the wall and then Ma will sure enough not be happy." Although her little sister annoyed her, Ruby did not like to see her get switched.

"Tomorrow is Ma's birthday and the paymaster is supposed to come today. So, I was thinking, we could ask Pa to let us go to the sutler's with him and get her a present. Mamie told me last night that she was going to bake her a cake." Rebecca gave the air one more kick and hopped to the ground, ready to go plead with her Pa.

"Now, Bec I think we should get her something small. Then, since Pa paid us last week to help clean the barracks, we could use our own money. That way the gift would really be from us." Ruby had heard her Pa say that stretching a paycheck for two months was harder than growing potatoes in West Texas with no rain. The paymaster was only able to make the rounds every other month to allot the salaries. The soldiers could charge only one half of a month's salary at a time; so, careful planning was a must.

"That's a great idea Rube, maybe we can even buy her some of that fancy soap she likes so much!" With the plan intact, the two sisters exited the kitchen building in search of their Pa. Rebecca was most excited, as she had not yet been allowed to make the trip for supplies.

They found their Pa bidding their Uncle Jeff good-bye before he started back on the trail. His job was to search for the renegades, Indians who refused to move to reservation land and continually killed and raided the white settlers. He then reported back to various fort commanders with information on the location of the troublemakers. Rebecca and Ruby hugged their uncle with tears in their eyes. Rebecca had not ever told anyone, but she was always a little afraid he would come back with a woman and would not have time for her anymore. Ruby's tears were shed for a different reason; she knew just how dangerous her uncle's duty was. Gemes put his arms around his daughters' shoulders and squeezed them close to him. He knew that his brother's departure was every bit as hard on them as it was on him.

The sutler's building was located a few miles down the creek from the fort. The wagon creaked past the Indian camps with Rebecca watching anxiously, hoping for a glimpse of Little Running Water. She had not seen him for two weeks and really wanted her frog. At least that was the reason she told herself she wanted to see him.

After all, boys were yucky and not good for anything except mischief. She hoped that Little Running Water had taken good care of her pet for her. She would just have to scalp him if he did not!

"Bec, it's not polite to stare. The way you're gawking, you'd think you've never seen a Comanche before." Gemes scolded his daughter as they made their way past the last group of tipis. The Indians would be in the area at least through the summer. He had promised Red Horse some more time to consider the offer of the land on the Brazos. If the tribe made the move, they would need to get there and get settled before the harshness of winter caught them. He noticed that some of the other tribes that had joined them for council were taking down their lodgings and preparing to move.

Rebecca felt a wave of disappointment at not seeing Little Running Water. However, her sadness was short-lived when she saw the sutler's building as they topped the knoll of the hill. Rebecca had a hard time walking calmly beside her father; she wanted to rush up the steps and explore. The outside of the hut was similar to the rest of the structures in the fort, but the inside was a vast array of colors. The aroma of various spices wafted through the air and tickled her nostrils.

Rebecca stopped to examine a row of damask tablecloths and almost fainted when she realized that they cost three dollars each. That amount was more than Pa made in a day! She held her and Ruby's money tightly in her fist. Her sister had chosen to stay with Mamie and help make the cake. Rebecca wished she were here to share the excitement. She noticed the dresses hanging on the far wall and decided dreaming did not cost anything. The sutler carried ready-made garments instead of ordering bolts of fabric, since few women were able to bring more than meager sewing supplies for mending. Occasionally, he did order some material for those like her Ma that had been fortunate enough to arrive with her sewing needs.

The Captain purchased cheese, berries, raisins, apples, sugar and spices, bread, butter, and jam. The sutler was an employee of the army and was required to provide adequate nourishment for the men. The issue of malnutrition among the soldiers had recently been a topic of hot debate in Washington. Gemes delighted in the knowledge that he would get to share the news with the women when he returned home. The results of the new legislation had actually reached them!

Meat was in ample supply at the fort. The area teemed with deer, buffalo, rabbits, and other wildlife, but gardening was next to impossible. First, the soldiers did not have the time to cultivate the land. Then, the lack of steady rain created harsh growing conditions. The fort did house some chickens and a few hogs, which were saved for special occasions. He knew that Eliza and Samantha had missed many of the luxuries from the store in Tennessee, although neither of them ever complained. His precious wife was as kind and good hearted as his mother had been.

"Pa, do you think I should buy Ma some fancy soap or a new pair of gloves?" Rebecca felt suddenly doubtful about her choice. She knew that the twenty-five cents in her pocket would only buy the soap, but somehow it did not seem to be a special enough gift for her Ma. She hoped Pa would buy her the gloves.

"Well, Bec, I'll tell you what. You and Ruby can buy

her the soap and I will buy her a new dress. Your Uncle Jeff left me the money to add a pair of gloves to her presents." Gemes felt a wave of loneliness overwhelm him. He would not ever get used to the idea of his brother having to travel and serve the army in the most dangerous position.

Rebecca smiled in delight and followed her Pa to the counter to pay for their purchases. Gemes was one of the few employees of the fort that did not have an ongoing charge account. Occasionally, he had been forced to put a few items on credit. However, since he was the commanding officer, his money usually supplied their needs and a few wants. He did have to be careful with his salary though. No one in the army got rich. Most of his soldiers were forced to charge supplies before the paymaster made his appearance each time. He had done his best to discourage them from wasting their pay on liquor, but the loneliness of their lives forced them to make unwise choices. Some of the soldiers had families that depended on them for financial support too, adding to the burdens of their existences.

The sutler, Warren P. Aldridge, stood behind the counter, patiently waiting for the selections to be made and assisting his customers when needed. His drooping mustache made him look like he was frowning, even when he smiled. He wore a business suit and a string tie. He was not much over five feet tall and had a little, round belly. Rebecca thought he looked like a nice enough man.

"I'll add a piece of rock candy for the little miss today." The sutler had enjoyed watching Rebecca's enthusiasm of her first trip to his place of business. He flashed a smile in her direction and noticed the unique color of her eyes. They sparkled with energy and made him wonder what she was thinking.

"Much obliged sir. I reckon you'll be busy all day. I asked my men not to all come see you at once, but they're mighty eager to see if you have any real food for them. I suspect they won't be disappointed." Gemes bade the merchant good day as he and Rebecca began to load the wagon. The

The mules, hitched to the wagon, were not as fast as horses, but were a lot less likely to be stolen by the Comanche. Riding horses out in the open was like holding candy out to a baby. An Indian's wealth and stature was judged by the number of horses he possessed, and stolen horses were, perhaps, more valuable than purchased ones. Therefore, the army required that the horses only be ridden on duty in and near the fort.

As the wagon rolled in front of the house, Samantha watched from the front porch. She had big news to share tonight and hoped that her family would be as excited as she was. She also hoped that Rebecca and her father had enjoyed a pleasant outing together. Gemes' job kept him busy most of the time, and she knew the girls missed the play time that they had shared with him before their move. Now, all of them had to stay alert and work hard just to survive.

"Hey Ma! Guess what? I got to see where the Comanche live up close! They sure got a lot of horses. Wonder where they buy 'em?" The captain and his wife exchanged a knowing look before Samantha reminded Rebecca, once more, to watch her speech. She did not know if she would ever teach her to speak properly, but then she was surrounded by bad examples. Samantha started to explain to her daughter that the horses were probable mostly the property of the United States government, but decided not to squelch her excitement of the day.

One of the soldiers crossed the yard to help unload the supplies. He was snickering to himself, because he had heard Rebecca's comments and question. She brought continuous laughter to the barracks, as the men would share her antics with each other at night. The other children living at the fort were not allowed much freedom. The only places they were seen were near their huts or at the captain's quarters for school. Sometimes, he questioned the captain's reasoning in not being more protective. He probably knew the Comanche would bring Bec back if they caught her! He watched Rebecca join some of the other children at their hut and was glad, for once, she was not exploring.

That night, the family enjoyed a fresh, apple pie, some store-bought bread, and jam, along with fried buffalo meat. After the meal, Samantha was given her presents and marveled at how Gemes was always able to be so generous. He was better with money than anyone she had ever known, and had not ever failed to surprise her on her birthday. She was especially proud of the indigo plant Gemes had added to his purchases at the last minute. Now, she would be able to dye the girls' dresses and add color to her curtains with the blooms. She remembered the time that he had told her he was breaking horses for a man in Tennessee to help make the payment on their land. Although times had been tough, he had managed to make the land payment and buy her an expensive brooch. She felt undeserving of his attention and tried to equally return his love. Some men were doting to cover guilt, but Gemes had not ever given her cause to distrust him.

"Thank you so much!" She made sure she kissed her husband first and then turned to her children and Eliza. She knew that the cake had been extra work for her elderly servant and appreciated the effort as much as the gifts.

"Now, I have a surprise for all of you." She made them wait a few excruciating seconds before she explained, "The Lord and I will be adding another blessing to this family around Christmas. I have known for some time, but after losing the last baby, I wanted to be sure this time before I told you." She explained, beaming, and then waited for her family's response.

"I's knowed it! I's done tol' my frien's that you'd be havin' us another youngun'. You's jus be wantin' to keep me hoppin'! Maybe now's you's can give Mistuh Gemes a lil boy." Mamie exclaimed in delight as she had been hoping for another Blair namesake as much as the men in the family; although, she would never trade her girls for anything.

"And here I thought she was just getting' fat!" Gemes playfully grabbed his wife and kissed her while his girls squealed with delight.

"He can sleep with me when he's old enough." Rebecca offered as she continued bubbling with excitement. Babies were a breath of hope in a desolate land where one problem seemed to follow another.

"Ma, I think Uncle Jeff will not be happy that you waited until he left to tell us." Ruby expressed her concern, knowing what her uncle's reaction would be.

"Actually, he guessed my secret before he left, and I decided I had better go ahead and tell all of you. So, he already knows, and he is very happy." Samantha announced coyly.

"So, my little brother figured it out before I did. I reckon he's one up on me now, but I do have some time to think about getting even now, don't I?" Gemes responded with a mischievous smile as he continued to hug his wife.

The evening continued with an unbearable heat and the inhabitants of Fort Chadbourne began to wish for cool fall air to take its place. August was near and often brought the most miserable weather of the year. Wet sheets hung in front of open windows to allow a breeze to blow through them and cool the homes. The Tennessee natives that had come from the hills had an especially difficult time adjusting. Somewhere close to midnight, the temperature finally began to drop and ease everyone into sleep, except Eliza.

The dream kept coming to her, more vividly each time. She would see Gemes tied to a stump and the Comanche torturing him beyond belief. Then, she would see the cruel masters of her friends and family beating them until they bled. Finally, she awoke, sweat saturating her nightgown. She arose from her bed and knelt beside it. She prayed for the Lord to take every horrible memory from her and help her to truly forgive. She knew that deep down in her heart, she must have lingering fear and hatred or these nightmares would not haunt her. She had preached forgiveness to those she had raised, but somehow she had not ever completely let go of her own anger.

The next morning, Eliza woke with a new spring in her step. She felt ten years younger and practically skipped to the kitchen house. She whistled a tune as she prepared breakfast and felt more ready for the day than she had in a long time.

"Did you sleep well Mamie?" Ruby asked, noticing the change in her caretaker. She, like her parents, had been concerned about Eliza's health.

"Yes, Miss Ruby, I did. You's see, sometime' the min' be needin' a lil sweepin' job. I got rid o' me some cobwebs." She explained her experience to the girl.

"Mamie sometimes you say things I don't understand, but maybe I will someday." She responded with a smile.

"Yes, chil' someday, someday....."

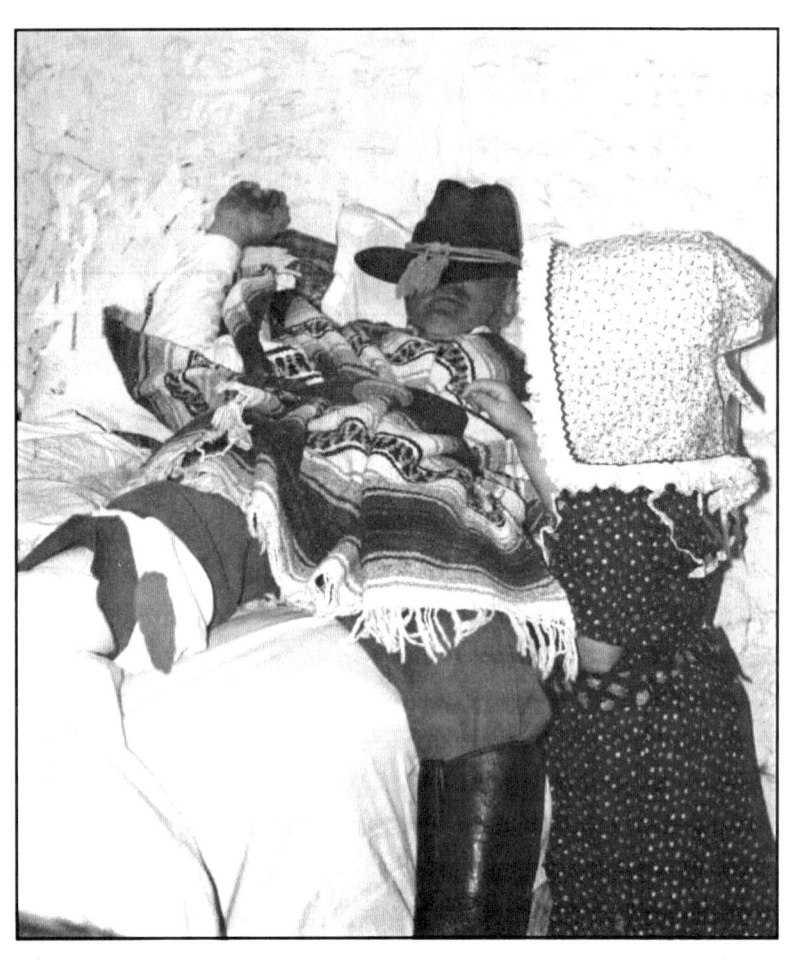

CHAPTER FOUR

ANOTHER CLOSE CALL

The August heat wave had left the coarse grass dryer than usual, bringing twenty straight days of temperatures above one hundred degrees. Even the snakes stayed in the shade for most of the daylight hours. Jeff reined his horse when he caught sight of the Colorado River. He had been scouting since mid-July and wanted desperately to be back at the fort before the September Comanche Moon. He removed his 50-caliber Sharps rifle from across his lap and lowered himself to the ground.

As he made his way to the water, Jeff began to feel uneasy and stayed alert for any signs of danger. He had not ever quite gotten used to the sense of vulnerability that he experienced when he was alone in the open country. Mesquite trees and cedars had not yet been introduced to Texas, and the Oak Trees only grew near rivers and streams. He removed his bedroll from his horse and both man and animal began to drink. Jeff took good care of his horse and gun, knowing they were his only allies against his enemies.

As Jeff began to take long, slow strokes in the water, he tried to imagine West Texas covered in towns. He could not fathom such a scene. The land seemed to require a lonely existence. He truly did not understand the government wanting to settle country with such unexpected twists and turns. With all the danger, however, at times, a feeling of serenity came, and Jeff felt as if this land was his and disliked the idea of the masses taking control. He knew this land and cherished it and could almost understand the Comanche wanting to keep it for their own.

After the refreshing swim, Jeff made his way to the tree, dressed and began to make camp for the night. He had not felt this relaxed in days. His horse shared his sentiments and began to nuzzle him playfully.

Jeff was enjoying his moments of peace so much that the rattlesnake caught him off guard. The fangs were already deep in his leg before he knew what was happening. Almost instantly, a severe stinging sensation began to radiate through his calf muscle. As panic began to seize his chest, he forced himself to stay calm. He lowered himself to the ground and searched for his knife in his bedroll.

Jeff wished for some whiskey to dull the pain as he slashed his skin above the fang marks. Poison began to slowly ooze from the bite. His leg was already swollen to the point of crippling him. He stared at his horse and had no idea how he would make it onto his back. As Jeff contemplated his fate, the horse lowered himself to the ground right next to his owner. Jeff stared in amazement and then carefully rolled himself onto the animal. The horse slowly rose to a standing position and then began to carefully make his way south, headed straight for the fort.

About two miles north of Fort Chadbourne, the Comanche were enjoying their nightly games. Red Horse sat near the fire and watched as the young and old alike enjoyed the rewards of his kill. Most of the time, the hunts were well planned and included a group of warriors. Today, Red Horse had wanted an excuse to be alone and had opted to go on a small hunt by himself. He knew that change was a part of life and he could predict the demise of those like Chief Yellow Wolf.

As a young brave, Red Horse had sworn to fight for the way of the Comanche and not ever let the white man force the Indian from his land. Now, life had altered his views. He had come to realize that life was what he made it. In Texas, as in any land, there were advantages and disadvantages. He also knew that the white man had the knowledge and weapons to win the battle. His people would be in better shape if they would cooperate and try to live in harmony with the white man.

Red Horse had known the betrayal of leaders who did not keep their word and had no trouble lying to the Comanche. Yet, since he had camped near Ft. Chadbourne, Red Horse had learned of another kind of man. Captain Blair had not ever led him astray. His words meant something, and he had not ever tried to trick the Indians. At the last council meeting, something strange had happened. Before leaving the fort, Red Horse had gotten a good look at the captain. There was something familiar, something stirring about his gaze. He had decided that the captain and his little friend from the creek must be related. Their eyes were the same color.

While the camp was celebrating the feast and enjoying fresh deer meat, Prairie Flower had taken advantage of the opportunity to seek solitude in the few trees by the creek. She had loosened her hair from its braids and her feet were bare. As she walked to the water, she thought about the conversation she had overheard between her brother and the elders of the tribe. He had encouraged continued peace with the white man since there finally appeared to be a captain that could be trusted. Her brother had a strange kind of wisdom, and she was surprised that the elders in the tribe listened to him. Yet, experience had taught her that Red Horse was usually right in his thinking.

The pounding of the horse's hooves startled the Indian woman out of her reverie. She saw that a semi-conscious man was barely clinging to the horse. No saddle was in place, and she knew something bad had happened. The horse stopped when he saw her and stood awaiting her help. After swiftly running to the pair, she quickly lowered the man to the ground and ran to find Red Horse.

Jeff lay on the ground, only vaguely aware of two feminine hands that had helped ease him off his horse. He felt his leg throbbing as he drifted in and out of consciousness. The swelling and purple discoloring had spread to his entire lower leg and was slowly inching its way up his limb. The poison had left him feeling unbearable hot and the August heat provided him no comfort. He vaguely remembered being bitten and had no idea how he had managed to remount his ride or how he had gotten nearly to Fort Chadbourne.

Red Horse ran behind his little sister, trying to keep up with her. The members of their tribe often teased that she was unmarried because no one could catch her. She raced to the spot where she had left the injured scout, knowing that time was of the essence.

Red Horse lowered himself to the ground and knelt beside the scout. He could tell that the man had been bitten and that without immediate care would die. He recognized the scout and felt a surge of panic come over him. He searched inside the pockets of the uniform for a knife and found none. Then, he spotted the slash marks and oozing venom on the man's calf and suspected he must have dropped his knife and weapon after the attack. He sent his sister back to the camp for help. The man was broad-shouldered and tall, and Red Horse knew that he would need help getting him back to his tipi.

Red Horse decided that it would be more merciful to carry the man back to camp rather than attempt to drape him back on the horse. He ordered the braves to roll him onto the buffalo robe, which Prairie Flower had retrieved, and make the transport. The trip was difficult and painstaking; yet, Red Horse was adamant about getting this white man help. The braves cast each other grumbling looks but knew better than to utter a sound of discontent.

Prairie Flower kept a constant vigil all through the night and would coax him to drink the tea the medicine woman had brought. The Comanche had learned the use of snakeweed as an antidote and many lives had been saved. He still felt feverish, but as the sun began to appear on the horizon, she noticed that the swelling was ceasing to spread. Her cheeks hurt from having to suck as much poison as she could from his leg. She spat at the ground, once more tasting the bitterness of the venom while Red Horse watched her from the opening of the tent.

Red Horse had known a special kind of friendship with his siblings since a war with the Sioux had left them orphans. Being the oldest of the clan, Red Horse, at thirteen years old, had taken full responsibility for his younger brothers and sisters.

Prairie Flower was the youngest girl, and he had felt a special burden for her. Her striking beauty had turned many eyes, but she was especially bashful and made no advances toward the men. In traditional Comanche custom, the women had the duty to show interest and begin the pursuit. There was somewhat of a game that was expected to take place. The courting was to be done secretly with both interested parties doing the flirting.

As the young lady knelt over her patient, her older brother wondered why she took such and interest in this white man. Maybe her compassionate nature was just causing her to feel sympathetic toward him or maybe she just wanted something special in trade. He knew that she feared white men and had not ever spoken to one, which was an unaccepted act anyway. Red Horse stood, as a proud father, admiring the beauty of his sister's fluid motions. She performed her tasks with skill, elegance, and grace. Her gentle fingers tended to her patient and her brow was knitted in concern. Her dress had been made with the same talented hands, and her braids were done tightly and neatly. A bright ribbon intermingled wtih the straight, black hair, adding to her already, unrefined beauty.

Red Horse moved to Prairie Flower's side and informed her that they must move the white scout back to his people. He had several braves standing outside the tent waiting to help make the transport. Prairie Flower frowned at her brother and leader. She did not like the white man's clothing of which he had grown so fond. The garments looked strange and made her feel as if her brother was somehow denying his culture.

Before being moved, Jeff was handed a pipe to smoke, packed with a medicinal herb. He attempted to sit, but Red Horse motioned him to lie back on his bed. Then, the chief knelt, cradled the scout's head, and assisted him in puffing on the pipe.

The braves had fixed a travois behind one of their horses. The carrying device consisted of two straight tree branches with a tanned buffalo hide stretched between them. A leather harness connected the travois to the horse. The ends of the branches drug the ground as they had no wheels.

Although the trip was only a mile long, Jeff felt every rock they crossed. He became extremely grateful for the medicine he had been given, knowing that otherwise, he could not have stood the pain. During his time as an Indian scout, he had come to admire their knowledge of the land, especially their use of natural plants and herbs for a variety of needs.

Gemes saw the small group of Comanche entering the main yard of the fort as he headed inside the house for breakfast. He spotted the travois behind one of the horses and noticed that the visitors were making their way to the surgeon. He stuck his head inside the door and told his wife that he was needed at the hospital. Gemes had a premonition that something had happened to one of his soldiers, since the Indians usually took care of their own.

The stench of disinfectant made its way into Jeff's nostrils as he was carried into the building. He knew by the smell that they had finally made it to the hospital. He tried to summon a smile for Doctor Jesse Denson. The post surgeon had been a friend of Jeff's long before they had met at Fort Chadbourne, both being Tennessee natives. The doctors goatee was sprinkled with grey, and his spectacles were perched on his nose.

The Comanche were known for their superior riding skills and rode quickly from the fort in true fashion. Gemes watched them leave as he walked toward the hospital. In the past, he had seen them riding under their horses' bellies and shooting their guns with extreme accuracy. He wiped the sweat from his brow and removed his hat before entering the front room.

"Gemes, I'm over here." The weak, male voice called to his older brother in relief. Jeff had never in his life felt so comforted to see someone. Even with the pain-relieving herbs, the ride to the fort had been excruciating. He had fainted several times during the short ride, that had seemed much longer.

"Jefferson Davis Blair, who'd you make mad this time?" Gemes tried hard to mask his concern as he attempted to joke by copying one of Mamie's often used phrases. She had accused Jeff of making someone mad anytime he came to her injured.

"Well, a very large rattler that wanted my leg for revenge and I suspect he got part of it too." Jeff's voice waned to a whisper as he slipped into unconsciousness.

The captain crossed the room to the fireplace where Dr. Denson stood disinfecting his surgical knife in the fireplace. Gemes noticed that since coming to West Texas, the surgeon's hair had begun to turn gray. The stressful life on the frontier had drastically aged the forty-year old man. He was expected to perform amputations in two to three minutes since pain medicine was severely limited, and many men and women had died from the intensity of the operations.

"Doc, is he going to make it?" Gemes kept his voice low in case his little brother woke and heard him talking.

"The Comanche did a fair job of getting him on the road to recovery. I'd say he has a better chance than most do with a snakebite." The surgeon turned to the captain, trying to keep any doubt out of his voice. He knew that the commanding officer had few soft spots and his little brother was one of them.

"What'd they do for him?" Gemes had an avid interest in Comanche ideas as he had seen many successes with their medical treatments.

"Well, they gave me some leaves and pointed to the water basin and told me to "make drink." So, I figured they expected me to make a tea out of the plant. They probably have been giving him some of the concoction since they found him. I wonder if these leaves are what I've heard Red Horse refer to as snakeweed." He held the mysteries plant parts in his hand and showed them to the captain.

"Let me look at those. Mamie used some leaves for a tea one time when a scorpion got a hold of me. Maybe this is the same stuff." He took the plants and examined them. "As a matter of fact, I think they are. Do you mind if I take a leaf to Mamie and ask her?"

"Not at all. We may have just found our antidote for rattlesnake bites. Evidently, it grows out here somewhere. Too bad we didn't have it back in April when Lieutenant Dearen met his fate." The surgeon would not ever understand why some good men were spared while others weren't.

"Will you have to perform an operation on his leg?" Gemes was concerned that his brother might lose the lower part of his limb.

"I'll need to open it up a bit more. Right now, it needs to drain as much as possible. Since, the Comanche gave him such good care, we may just be able to save his life and his leg." The doctor sounded very optimistic.

Rebecca did not sleep at all that night. Her Ma had refused to let her go see her uncle until morning. By the time Gemes had returned to his quarters, the sun had long since disappeared into the night sky. Samantha was absolutely not going to let her eight-year old little girl go traipsing around with rattlesnakes and Comanche controlling the dark.

Before Samantha had time to stop her daughter, Rebecca had left the house and was running toward the hospital. She did not stop for a breath until she stood in front of the door. She opened the door as quietly as she could and tiptoed inside. She wished she had thought to bring her uncle some biscuits from breakfast, and then quickly remembered that the surgeon's wife was an excellent cook.

"Hi Bec, thought I needed a little supervision, huh?" Nothing cheered Jeff Blair anymore than seeing his niece. She stood, timidly, beside his bed. That morning, she had been extra careful with her hair and clothes; she wanted to look nice for her uncle.

"Uncle Jeff, Pa told me what happened? Does it hurt terribly?" Her little lip quivered as she stared down at her uncle. His cot looked very uncomfortable. She wished he could stay at the house with them, but Ma had said he needed to be at the hospital for awhile.

"Now Bec you stop that worrying. Remember, Mamie always says that worrying isn't faith." He tried to calm her fears. "Besides, I'm going to be just fine. The Comanche took good care of me before they brought me home. I sure am glad Yellow Wolf didn't find me. I'm not sure how far I rode before Red Horse's bunch rescued me, but I do know that Mamie's angels must have been working again."

"Mamie's angels are always on duty when you're awake." Rebecca teased her uncle as she realized that he was not dying.

"Do you see what that rattler did to my leg?" Jeff motioned to his swollen limb that the surgeon had elevated with blankets. Poison continued to seep from the wound although the discoloration had somewhat diminished.

Rebecca's eyes grew big, and she thought how very painful the injury must be. Once more, she choked back tears, and she leaned forward to kiss her uncle on the forehead. As she left the building and started down the steps, the sobs escaped her.

Dr. Denson watched the child from the window. He started to go outside and comfort her, but knew that the Blairs preferred to deal with their problems privately. He had been relieved that morning when the captain had said that Mamie assured him the weed the Comanche brought was indeed the weed she knew to be an antidote against poison.

The cry made Rebecca feel better, and she started toward her house knowing her uncle was going to be okay. She decided she would find him a present and bring it to him later. Maybe, he would like to have a pet frog too.

"How was your uncle?" Samantha asked her daughter as she found her place at the table. Rebecca's eyes were red from crying and her Ma knew that the visit had been upsetting. She took her hand and gently stroked the side of her daughter's cheek in a comforting gesture.

"He's going to be just fine. Thanks to the Comanche." Rebecca tried to sound positive and not let anyone know she was the least bit worried.

Samantha stiffened at the mention of the Indians and withdrew her hand. "What do the Comanche have to do with anything?" She questioned.

"Didn't Pa tell you? They gave him some kind of special tea to drink and brought him here for help." Rebecca had overheard her Pa talking to one of the soldiers while she had tried to go to sleep. Samantha had gone to bed soon after supper on Mamie's insistence since the new life growing inside of her took much of her energy. So, Gemes had not had a chance to provide her with many details.

"Now, Rebecca, I hope you didn't tire your Uncle Jeff with a bunch of questions." Samantha tried to change the subject. She was still not comfortable with the increasing interaction at the fort with the natives.

"Don't worry Ma, I didn't. Anyway he went back to sleep before I could say much. Besides, when he was awake, he was too busy teasing me for me to ask him questions. Do you think snakebites hurt real bad?" She looked at her mother with childlike innocence.

"Rebecca, I think they are probably painful, but I also know that if anybody can survive a rattler, it's your Uncle Jeff." She forced a smile on her face and lifted her fork to her mouth. The rest of the meal was spent discussing everyone's plans for the day.

After the table had been cleared, Gemes wrapped his arm around his wife and assured her that Jeff stood a good chance of surviving and keeping his leg. He also apologized for not having time to give her more details earlier. Samantha thought, once more, how fortunate she was to have married into such a strong, yet gentle family.

"Mamie, why does Ma always talk about something else anytime I mention the Comanche?" Rebecca asked the servant as they washed the clothes later that morning. A cool breeze had broken the heat as the hope of Fall made its appearance. The elderly woman did not lift her eyes from the washtub, and Rebecca thought at first that she was ignoring her. The piece of cloth that encased the servant's head partially shielded her face from the girl's speculative gaze.

Finally, she responded, "Now, Miss Bec I 'spect she be mite near like mos' fol'. She be havin' some fear she be needin' to let the good Lord take care of. But don' you be worryin' yoself none, someday she be lettin' all go. Someday....you's jus' wait an' see." Eliza began to hang the wash on the line with someday in mind.

CHAPTER FIVE

COMANCHE MOON

Red Horse squatted beside the fresh grave. He and one other brave had stayed to continue working on the rocks while the others returned to camp. Comanche graves became a work of art. Rocks were neatly chipped to form a fairly smooth, round basin. A narrow channel cut in the rocks lead away from the rim of the basin to carry off the surplus water. The deceased were buried with souvenirs from their lives, keeping with their superstitious nature.

While the two men worked, they began to discuss the change in the weather. September brought the growing moon and was the preferred time for raids. While Red Horse and his tribe were trying to make peace with the white man, Yellow Wolf and his gang were continually raiding all over South Texas. Sometimes, the renegades made their way further north, much too close to Fort Chadbourne for Red Horse's liking.

Red Horse had endured much stress to see the results he was now experiencing. Dealing with the white man had been a relatively easy task compared to coping with the pride and stubborness of his fellow Comanche. He did not want Yellow Wolf's rebellion to destroy his relations at the fort.

The day prior to the death of one of the elders, Red Horse had been reminded of past massacres. Cynthia Ann Parker had been seen begging for food at the fort. She was a white woman that had been captured as a young teenager in a cruel raid. She had married a Comanche and became a true Indian. When she was later rescued, she had lost her mind. Now, she was neither Comanche nor white and wandered, aimlessly from place to place, without hope.

Red Horse knew that one raid led to retaliation from soldiers and one retaliation from soldiers led to another raid. The cycle had to be broken someday or the blood shed would not cease. While he could understand the unfairness in the plight of the Comanche, he knew that the nation was fighting a lost cause. He only hoped that Yellow Wolf's actions would not cost him the peace he had fought so hard to find.

The brave assisting the council chief listened to Red Horse's concerns with mixed emotions. While he felt jealous that a man younger than him had achieved such an esteemed position in the tribe, he also had come to respect and admire his leader. He knew Red Horse had strong magic and that those who opposed him usually met a terrible fate.

The two men finished their task and made their way back to camp. Prairie Flower had been watching the hospital from her view on the bank of the creek. She quickly turned her eyes from the fort to the river, hoping her brother would not guess the direction of her thoughts. While he had grown to respect the officers in the fort, she felt he would disapprove of her interest in the scout. She left the river and returned to camp to finish her day's work.

One large Oak tree stood behind the commanding officer's quarters. Samantha had assumed the role of teacher at the fort since no school was available. Occasionally, when the weather was nice, she would allow the children to follow her to the base of the large tree. She enjoyed teaching them under the shade as it provided a break from the mundane rhythm of her house. This particular September day, Edward Guess had raised his hand and asked if the class might read under the tree. Samantha felt the cool breeze through the window and the beautiful Fall air beckoning to her. She agreed that today would be perfect for studying outdoors.

Rebecca was elated to escape the confines of the front room. The stiff chairs surrounding the table dug into her muscles, and the discomfort increased on beautiful days when she would rather be exploring. Her Ma had the extra burden of being a parent and educator. Before she had married her Pa, she had taught school in a small Tennessee community. She had become skilled in dealing with children; so, she did not have much trouble, except when Rebecca decided to have fun.

As the grammar rules were reviewed and practiced, Rebecca found her eyes searching the grass for any kind of excitement. She wore her school dress, freshly dyed from her Ma's new Indigo plant. Rebecca detected a slight movement coming from the tall grass a few yards from them, but decided it was just the wind blowing. Her mother sent a stern look her way, and Rebecca once more focused her attention on learning. She did not enjoy the grammar lesson; she personally thought the way her Mamie talked sounded just fine!

As the lecture continued, the children became more aware of their surroundings and less aware of their lessons. Samantha, herself, was finding concentration difficult on such a perfect day. As she contemplated releasing the class early, something jumped inside her long skirt.

She did a dance and tried frantically to get the slimy creature out of her clothes. The children's laughter rang across the grassy plain as their teacher performed a funny little jig for them.

"Rebecca Jane Blair! Is this your frog? I thought I told you to get rid of him!" Samantha seldom yelled at her girls, and Rebecca knew that she was in for a good switching if she did not think fast. She was also a little concerned about her mother's condition.

"To tell you the truth, Ma, I lost my frog a few days after I found him." She told a partial truth. She really was not sure this frog and her Benjamin Franklin were one in the same or exactly where her new Indian friend had been keeping him. She did think she could see Little Running Water sprinting back to his side of the river though and felt a more than a little guilty.

"Since I can't prove you were at fault here, I won't punish you this time. But, I had better not EVER see you with another animal in our house. Do I make myself clear?" She gave Rebecca a look that meant business.

"Yes, ma'am!" Rebecca's promise was sincere, at least right at that moment.

From his perch on the hospital porch, Jeff had witnessed the entire scene. As much as he loved his sister-in-law, he felt she was way too strict with Rebecca at times. He burst into laughter at the same time as the children. He had watched the little Comanche boy make his way through the grass. He had suspected he meant to play a prank on the group in true Comanche fashion. While this particular tribe had brought little mischief, some of the children delighted in playing jokes on each other and youngsters of the fort. Now, he wondered if he and Rebecca knew each other. He remembered her having a frog and had a strange inkling the two had met. He just had not discovered the how and where, but he was determined to do so.

As he sat trying to piece together the pieces of the puzzle in his mind, he was being watched. Prairie Flower sat on her usual perch and gazed at a thick head of blond hair. Her coal black hair was hanging in a braid down her back. She longed to see those bright, blue eyes when they were not full of pain. She wondered if he was kind like the commander, or if he bore the usual hatred she had so often experienced from the white man. Her life was full of hard work since the Comanche women did most of the labor while the men hunted, slept, or planned wars.

The rest of the day, the cavalry rode in uniform around the fort in increasing numbers. Security would remain increased until the month ended. So far, Yellow Wolf had stayed to the south, but could not be trusted to remain there. The Texas flag and the United States flag were carried by two different soldiers; Texas was the only state whose flag held equal importance to the nation's flag. The former independent nation lived by its own set of rules.

The afternoon grew late and evening chores began. Jeff had grown tired of sitting on the porch and decided he was now strong enough to walk to Gemes' quarters. He slowly began to make his way through the tall grass. The first few steps were relatively pain free, but the further he went, the discomfort began to surface. By the time he had reached the front steps of his brother's house, he had sweat pouring down his face.

"Jefferson Davis Blair, I's oughta be a switchin' you's

good now! Jus' what do's you's thin' you's be tryin' t' do?" Eliza hurried down the steps to assist the grown man she would not ever by through trying to raise.

"Mamie, I had all of that stinking hospital I could stand. Besides, I think Bec was going to drive Doc Denson out of his mind with her questions if I didn't hurry up and get out of there!" He attempted to laugh, but a sharp pain stopped the sound before it reached his throat.

Ruby and Rebecca raced onto the porch, panicking at the sight of their uncle in so much pain. "Uncle Jeff, are you okay?" Ruby stepped forward and assisted Eliza in supporting her uncle.

"If he is, he ain't gonna be when Mamie and Ma get through with him." When Rebecca wanted to be emphatic, proper English just did not seem to get the job done. She stood with her hands on her hips in apparent disapproval of her uncle's behavior. She acted as if she was personally in charge of him.

"Now, I think Bec just might be right. Surviving a rattler's an easy task compared to warding off feisty women." He winked at his nieces while Mamie pretended to scowl at him.

As Jeff was escorted into the house, he thought about just how much love his family shared. They had all been through the fire and had come through it with scars, but their unusual bond had created pillars of strength out of all of them. While the women attempted to make him comfortable inside the front room, Jeff suddenly realized he had not seen the captain since early that morning. With September's growing moon, he did not like his brother's absence. He knew that there would not ever be enough distance for his comfort between him and Yellow Wolf.

He knew that nearby forts were experiencing raids and mischievous pranks. One of Yellow Wolf's favorite pastimes was leading a group of men into the white man's camp waving sheets at their horses. The animals would disappear. Most of them Yellow Wolf kept; a few would eventually find their way home.

Long after the evening meal had been served, the front door finally opened and Gemes returned. He hung his hat and crossed to the water basin in silence. As he washed his face, he felt the knowing stare behind him. When serious issues arose, the Blairs were people of few words, but not many were needed. They well knew how to read each other.

"Hello, Jeff. I guess you got tired of pestering Doc Denson, huh?" Gemes attempted to avoid any questions, all the while knowing his efforts were futile. Jeff would want to know every detail of where he had been and what he had been doing.

Before Jeff had time to quiz the captain, Samantha gracefully made her presence known. She began placing her husband's food on the table. He stopped her before she could leave him and his brother alone. He gently placed his arm around her shoulder, drawing him to her and gently placing a kiss on her lips. He paid no mind that they had an audience; he knew his wife needed to feel secure. September was a frightful time for all of them. She returned his embrace and said a silent prayer for her soulmate. Before leaving the room, she cast a concerned look in her brother-in-law's direction.

Gemes sat at the table and hungrily devoured the food. He cleared the table and rinsed the dishes before he uttered another word to Jeff. He scooted a chair closer to his brother's cot, which Mamie had fixed him, and sat to face the inevitable inquiries.

"So, are you going to tell me where you've been all day, or am I going to have to drag it out of you?" Jeff had a feeling his brother had been doing some scouting of his own.

"I reckon since where I've been concerns all of us, I might as well tell you. Do you think you could make it to the porch if I help you?" Gemes knew that there were way too many ears in his house for a private conversation. He did not wish to create any more anxiety among the members of his family.

"I expect I can since I made it all the way from the hospital to here by myself." Jeff was already standing before he finished his sentence. He hobbled beside his brother out onto the front porch.

The two men shared a few moments of silence as they stared into the clear September night. Jeff had lit his pipe and the smoke was circling around the top of his head. Gemes had his legs crossed on top of the railing and appeared not to have a care in the world.

"Red Horse and I did a little scouting of our own today," Gemes announced as if the event occurred every day.

"I reckon he fears Yellow Wolf about as much as most. Rumor has it that Yellow Wolf killed one of Red Horse's wives in a raid on their tribe. Red Horse had stolen over a dozen horses and Yellow Wolf was determined to have them. That hatred goes way back." Jeff had learned to speak a great deal of the Comanche language and his knowledge earned him extra information.

"That explains why he met me outside of camp today

and wanted to go with me. I can't say as I minded the extra protection of his warriors that followed us. They kept their distance, but they were definitely there. A Comanche's like a wolf; you can feel their presence from miles away." Gemes tensed as he removed his legs from the railing and leaned forward to look at his brother. He placed his hat on the back of the chair and ran his hands through his sandy hair and sighed.

"Does Red Horse still promise to provide us protection against Yellow Wolf if he decides to attack? I am surprised the elders of the tribe are backing him. Peace talks only go so far in war." Jeff had witnessed betrayals on both the part of the United States government agents and on the side of the Comanche. He had learned to be cautious in his expectations.

"That's what he guarantees. I'm not real sure what happened between him and Yellow Wolf, but there seems to be a mutual respect of boundaries. The one thing that does concern me, though, is if Yellow Wolf can totally control his own men. They are some of the fiercest fighting Comanche that I have ever seen and the best riders too. They can shoot as straight riding under a horse as they can on top. But then, so can Red Horse." Gemes began to breathe a prayer for the good Lord to get them through the rest of the bright September nights. He kept his long Kentucky rifle near him, just in case.

Jeff did not respond, as he knew that the only thing any of them could do was to stay alert and pray. If any Comanche took a notion to do something, he did it and nothing stopped him. They had already posted extra sentries around the fort. Jeff and Gemes watched them, the infantrymen carrying their long Mississippi rifles and the

Calvary on their horses with their carbine rifles resting on their laps.

Samantha rubbed her lower back and stretched. A strong kick from the baby told her that her spill had done him no damage. She had a feeling this little one was going to be a namesake. Mamie agreed with her and had been accurate in predicting the girls. So, Samantha began calling her expected blessing Joseph Curtis.

Gemes rose and kissed Mamie on the cheek before she made her nightly walk across the yard. The inhabitants of the fort had long since accepted the strange relationship between owner and servant. After her talk with Rebecca, Eliza felt unusually tired. The child's fear of the threats around her had grown in intensity over the last few days. Her Mamie had tried to soothe her with the success her Pa had known with Red Horse and his band. Rebecca was not easily fooled though, and new that chiefs like Yellow Wolf continued to pose danger. Mamie had finally convinced her to say her prayers and leave her fears with God. Then, she had told her that someday she would not have to be afraid. Someday, the white man and the Comanche would cease to fight. Rebecca said she hated that word "someday." Then, she fell asleep.

CHAPTER SIX

STAMPEDE

September passed without incident at the fort. Security had returned to normal, and the boards were off the windows. The mothers, while less fearful, still kept close eyes on their children.

The supply wagon to the store had brought the sutler some potatoes. So, Mamie had decided to fix a meatloaf, mashed potatoes and gravy, and even baked a cake. She had been trying to put some flesh back on Jeff. Since his ordeal, he had lost so much weight that his uniform had to be altered.

Eliza watched the children, once again, having school underneath the tree. Gemes had taken his wife a chair to accommodate her growing figure and she now sat teaching her students. The boys and Rebecca fidgeted while the girls sat primly and properly. Samantha was explaining the rules of grammar to the younger students, and the older ones were working on essays.

Eliza was kneading bread dough when Jeff came into the room and announced, "Mamie, I think I'll venture out a ways and see if I spot Red Horse. I'd like to know more about what Yellow Wolf's been up to lately." That morning had been cold, but the afternoon was pleasantly warm. October was one of the mildest months of the year with the temperature usually averaging in the upper sixties.

"I's don' be thinkin' that be a wise idea. Now, do's you's. Why, it ain't been no time since that beast near took yo' life." She felt he was still way too weak to resume his duties. Right now, his mind was the strongest member of his body and would probably win the struggle.

"Now, Mamie, you know I can't sit still for long. Why do think I haven't found me a woman. I'm too fast to be caught. Nope, I just can't stay still for long. I gotta keep moving." He pulled a chair near the open kitchen door. As he made himself comfortable, he noticed that the cooler weather agreed with Mamie. The flushed look in her cheeks was gone, and she looked like she felt better than she had of late.

"You's bes' jus' forgit yo' wanderin' itch fo' the time bein'. You's not near so tough as you's be thinkin' now." She gave him one of her looks, hoping to persuade him to continue to rest for a bit longer.

"I won't go far, but if I don't ride, I'll never get the stiffness out of my joints." He was going absolutely stir-crazy. He ran a hand through his blond hair, squeezed his Mamie's shoulder, and left the kitchen. He limped across the yard to his horse, saddled it, and mounted with more than a little difficulty. The woman that had raised him watched from the kitchen window and sent another prayer into the heavens.

As Eliza was continuing her preparation of the evening meal, she spotted a few buffalo just over the hill to the south of the fort. She did not pay them much attention as the creatures were seen often. She had a fleeting thought of some fresh meat and then went about her afternoon's work. Samantha released the children from their lessons, and they scampered across the grass, celebrating their freedom.

Arizona Cain left her hut and walked toward the commanding officer's quarters. She had developed a close relationship with Samantha since her husband had been assigned to the fort. She was glad September was gone, and they all felt freer to do as they pleased. While their daily routines kept them from having much leisure time, the two women did enjoy occasional visits with each other. Today, Samantha was sitting on her front porch with a cup of coffee. She rose and greeted her friend.

"Would you like a cup of coffee? Mamie made a cake for supper, and she sliced us a piece for now." Samantha extended the invitation while Arizona tried to decide what to do with her four year old little boy.

"I would love a cup. I think I will fasten a rope to Stephen's suspenders and tie it to the tree. Then he can play while we visit and I won't have to worry about him wandering." While Arizona securely fastened her son to the tree, Samantha made her way into the house to retrieve the refreshments. When she returned with the snack, the two women settled themselves into the chairs on the porch and began to chat.

"I thought I saw Rebecca talking to one of the little Comanche boys during the last council that was held here. Has she learned some of their language?" Arizona had always been amazed by Rebecca's intelligence. She knew that both, Gemes and Samantha, had brilliant minds that their two girls had inherited.

"I expect she's picked up a few words here and there. I do hope that she'll stay far away from those Indians. I just don't trust them. I'll never understand why Gemes does. He acts as if their his best friends sometimes. He seems especially fond of the one they call Red Horse. It's terribly troubling to think how much confidence he places in him." Samantha adjusted her uncomfortable frame and worriedly shifted her gaze to the tipis she could see by the creek.

"Well, Samuel seems to thinks the captain knows what he's doing. He's always saying you should never argue with success. He also says that your husband has the heart of a dove and the constitution of a mule; so, the politicians and the Comanche know not to mess with him." Arizona giggled softly and took a sip of her coffee.

Samantha could not help but share a laugh with her friend. Her husband did have a kind heart and a strong will. His determined spirit was probably the reason he had survived his capture and later, overcome some huge obstacles in his life. She could not imagine how some women endured an unkind man, as she had not ever experienced cruelty.

"You're probably right, my friend. I just don't understand how he, of all people, would act so naive about the Comanche. They are still wild savages. Who knows when they will turn on us." Although Samantha was an unusually kind woman herself, a fear had devoured her, and she could not shake loose of it.

"Look Samantha!" Arizona suddenly leapt to her feet in panic. Headed straight toward the fort was a massive throng of pounding hooves. At least two hundred buffalo were stampeding quickly in their direction. The women ran for cover.

" Stephen, I forgot about Stephen!" She raced to the front door to retrieve her little boy. She could no longer see him under the tree, and she feared that he had been trampled. She stumbled into the front room of the officer's quarters and began to grieve the loss of her son. The herd of thundering beasts prevented her from rescuing his body.

Jeff had been on his way back to the fort when he felt the earth vibrating beneath him. He hurried his horse and was almost to the house when he spotted the child. Tears were streaming down his face and he was huddled as close as he could get next to the tree. Jeff ignored the ache in his leg and grabbed Stephen in his arms. Then, he quickly climbed the tree with a squirming child firmly in his grasp. All the while, the ground continued to tremble and shake under the mighty force of the powerful beasts. Panic had taken captive the entire fort. All the residents had sought cover and were huddled in balls of fear in various sanctuaries.

The earth continued to protest the weight of the thundering buffalo, and Jeff grasped a tree branch with one hand. Instinct kept him from dropping the child, despite the searing fire consuming his body. The pain became so intense that the scout thought he would faint. Dust billowed from the ground into his throat and nose, choking man and child.

The pounding of hooves reverberated for miles, resembling the force of an earthquake. One lone bull stood pawing the ground underneath the Oak tree that sheltered the scout and the little boy. His snorts were heard from the porch of the main house as Samantha and Arizona tried to catch a glimpse of Stephen's body. They expected to see a mutilated corpse. Finally, the animal decided to continue with the rest of the heard as he thundered off into the distance, sending more dust spiraling into the Texas air.

One side of a jackal hut was obliterated with a few

blows from powerful horns. Damage was being done to all of the unstable buildings. Even the stone structures were shaken, and some of their porches were destroyed. The few seconds that lapsed during the stampede seemed like an eternity.

From her side of the creek, Prairie Flower watched helplessly as Jeff struggled to cling to safety. She had watched him rescue the boy and make the escape. She whispered a word of hope into the air and waited for the onslaught to end. She hoped that the spirit world would help him and not punish her for wanting to break the tribe's tradition. She feared she had angered the gods. The buffaloes passed near the Indian camp and trampled a few tipis on the way. However, most of the damage had been done inside the boundaries of the fort.

Arizona stepped onto the porch, sobbing uncontrollably. She had been unable to reach the tree before the trampling animals had stopped her actions. She did not know how, but she was praying for a miracle. With tears streaming down her face, she quickly made her way to the tree, seeing no sign of her child. The rope was still tied to the tree and she followed its length up the trunk with her eyes. There, in the fork of the huge Oak tree were and unconscious scout and a very frightened little boy.

Samantha ran to her friend and followed the direction of her gaze. She froze when she saw her brother-in-law. His face was ashen, and he appeared to barely be breathing. She called frantically for Gemes, hoping that he was on his way to check on his family. Then, another thought of panic struck her. Where were her children and her husband? Were they safe?

"Samantha, are you okay?" She felt the gentle pressure of her husband's large hand on her shoulder.

"I'm fine, just shaken, but that's more than I can say for your brother. He passed out in the tree holding Stephen. I have no idea what he was doing out and about in the shape he is." She motioned to the spot where the man and child remained perched.

Gemes climbed the tree and handed the child to his mother, and then contemplated how he would get his solid brother safely to the ground. Before he could make a decision, several of his subordinates came running.

"What's the matter Captain? Is he all right? Do you need some help?" He was bombarded with questions and offers of assistance. Somehow he managed to dislodge Jeff from the branches and hand him to the soldiers waiting below the tree. Four men carried him into the front room of the house. The girls had returned home and Samantha sent Ruby to fetch the doctor. She quickly forgot her relief that her children were safe as fear for her brother-in-law took its place.

Samantha retrieved some extra pillows from the bedrooms and elevated Jeff's leg while Eliza began to bathe him in cool water from the basin. Gemes started pacing the floor, occasionally stopping to check his brother's pulse. Jeff showed no reaction and remained limp on the cot.

"What happened here? I knew he was not strong enough to be out and about on his own. He wouldn't listen; you know how he is when he gets restless." Doctor Denson shook his head in frustration and worry as he placed his black bag on the table. He suspected that a significant amount of poison remained in Jeff's bloodstream and had circulated throughout his body. His fears were confirmed as he began to examine his patient.

"I think the only hope for him is to try and find some of the weed the Comanche uses. It appeared to make a big difference initially. The only thing I can do for him is to make him another poultice and try to draw some more of the poison out of his leg. He will also need to be bathed often to keep his fever from rising. That's about all that can be done. However, we all know that saying a prayer or two wouldn't hurt anything." The doctor tried to offer some kind of hope after delivering the devastating news.

"Pa, Rebecca and I can go ask the Indian for some of that weed. We aren't afraid." Ruby spoke bravely surprising everyone. She had not shown any interest in associating with the Comanche like Rebecca had and tended to be fearful when they were in the confines of the fort.

Startled, the captain looked at his daughter proudly and responded, "Ruby, your offer is very generous. However, since I have made friends with Red Horse, I will go ask him for help. I need to talk to him about some other business anyway."

While Samantha was proud of her husband's accomplishments, she still could not help feeling unsettled when he referred to the chief as his friend. She did not comment knowing that her fears must be kept at bay in order to save her brother-in-law. She returned to his bedside as her husband and the doctor moved to the porch to visit in private.

After his chat with the doctor, the captain mounted his horse and made his way to the Indian camp. He normally used the mules if his was going to be passing the invisible line of safety, but at that particular moment he needed the security of the familiar. Besides, he had grown to trust Red Horse's people enough that he no longer feared that they might steal from him. He also believed that they offered him protection against the renegades. With one purpose in mind, horse and rider made their way across the creek.

Red Horse saw the rider quickly approaching the camp. He lifted his hand in greeting and uttered the Comanche term "chemakacho" meaning "the good white man." He could detect that something was drastically wrong by the countenance of his white counterpart. As Gemes walked toward the chief in greeting, a flood of memories poured into Red Horse's mind. He tried to keep his face expressionless, but the shock of what he was realizing overwhelmed him. The captain was the same little boy he had untied from that stump so long ago. Fate had brought them together for a purpose. What was it? He decided he must seek the answers from the spirit world.

"Chief Red Horse," Gemes returned the greeting. "My brother has once again turned ill. Will you help us? We need some more of the thing you call snakeweed. Maybe it will save him." Gemes kept his English simple and wondered if Red Horse was having trouble understanding the request. He wore a look of confusion and appeared shaken by something.

"Buffalo. Today they make much trouble." The chief acknowledged that he had understood. "Red Horse no rush animals. We think maybe Yellow Wolf. Red Horse find help for chemakacho. Come friend." He then went in search of his sister. She would know exactly where the weed was growing. She had always shown a fascination for healing people. Although she claimed not to want

81

the position of medicine woman, everyone in the tribe often looked to her for healing.

Red Horse released a rapid flow of his language to his sister. Usually, Gemes could understand a few of the Uto words, but today they were spoken too quickly and urgently. Prairie Flower scampered out across the cross and disappeared behind a hill. Red Horse stood quietly making no effort to further communication with the captain. Gemes could not decide what was wrong with him. He was acting very strangely and totally out of character. The personality shift greatly disturbed the officer.

Within a short period of time, Prairie Flower had returned with a large handful of weeds, proudly showing them to her brother and Captain Blair. Then, her countenance changed as the realization finally dawned that Jeff must be once again in trouble. She had overheard his name the day they had taken him to the hospital. Prairie Flower always listened closely to the white man anytime she had a chance, wanting to grasp every word she could of the fascinating new language.

Gemes gave Red Horse a new knife in exchange for the herbs. He knew that his soldiers would go berserk if they knew he had given a Comanche a weapon in trade, but he felt his brother was worth the risk. He knew the Comanche provided the only apparent hope for Jeff's recovery.

As Gemes made his way back to the fort, he remained puzzled over Red Horse's behavior. Did he stampede the buffalo to destroy them? Doubt would flood his mind, and then, he would rationalize it away. No, Red Horse's band had also been affected. As the captain had ridden into their camp, he had noticed that the Indians were busy fixing several tipis. They would not purposely rush the animals so near their own camp. Yet, there was definitely something strange about the way Red Horse had acted. The captain decided to increase security back to the level it had been during the Comanche moon.

Gemes sat alone on the front porch, wishing his younger brother were there to help him sort through his doubts. They had endured so many hardships together that they often solved problems better as a team. A lone tear slid down his cheek as he began to wonder if he would ever again share a conversation with Jeff.

Across the creek, Prairie Flower was shedding her own tears in the dark inside her tent. She must hide her sorrow from the other members of her tribe. They would ban her from their presence if they knew how deep her feelings had grown for the white scout. She had shared only a few words with him, but felt connected to him forever. Now, the spirit world was punishing her for her betrayal. She tossed restlessly on the buffalo hide, which she used for her bed, feeling as if her life had just lost its purpose.

Long after, everyone else had retired to their tipis, Red Horse sat outside his shelter contemplating his new knowledge. Should he hold a council and let the tribe elders know that the captain was the one with the special magic? Did he let the captain know who he was? He was uncertain of how to deal with this new information. Maybe he should get his pipe and see if he could travel into the spirit world. Maybe the spirits would reveal to him what he should do. Surely, someday, the captain would discover the secret. When would that someday be and what would become of them if Captain Blair learned the truth? Red Horse eased away from the camp to seek answers with the apprehension of someday weighing heavily on his thoughts.

CHAPTER SEVEN

PLANS CHANGE

The next morning, Red Horse called a council of the elders. He had decided not to reveal his part in the captain's escape but did feel a need to divulge his other concerns to the tribal leaders. The dawn had awakened him from a troubled, restless state of sleep. He had visions all night of disaster and believed the spirits were telling him to leave the area soon or certain destruction would come to the tribe. Decisions had to be made.

Red Horse had risen to his powerful position due to a combination of his leadership skills, his generosity and kindness to other members of the tribe, and his wisdom in council. His knowledge of the territory and common sense had made his nomination a surety. Also, he had acquired the ability to speak persuasively on matters of importance. The warriors obeyed the decisions of their elders from fear of angering the chiefs and displeasing the supernatural powers. Although many of the younger braves did not like the brotherhood Red Horse shared with the white man, they followed him out of a sense of obligation to the tribe. If any of them ever discovered Red Horse's moment of weakness, his days as council chief would be ended.

The piece pipe was passed between the men while they waited for the chairman or "primus inter pares" to begin the discussion. The urgent meeting had not surprised the members of the council. They knew that anytime disaster happened inside the fort, a portion of the residents was ready to blame the nearest Comanche. Distrust on both sides still existed.

The council began with Red Horse assuring the members that, after careful investigation, he had found no evidence of any of the young braves causing the mishap. He did feel, however, that Yellow Wolf being responsible was a strong likelihood. He spoke urgently in his native tongue. He had appeared in full tribal dress, deserting the white man's garments. At that moment, he wanted to be entirely Comanche to ensure the blessings of the spirit world.

After much discussion, the council decided to move the tribe no later than thirty moons from that day. The first snow did not usually come to the area until late December of early January; so, the tribe would have time to relocate before winter. West Texas did not experience the severity of the season like the northern states but did have some pretty cold weather and a few snowfalls. The tribe would need time to move and organize a hunt before all the wildlife also sought shelter, making fresh meat more difficult to find.

Prairie Flower was outside her tipi when her friend, Morning Dove, approached and asked her if she had heard the news. Both young women had discussed the reason for the called council earlier that day. Prairie Flower suspected that there had been grumblings in the white man's camp, placing blame on their band for the stampede. Morning Dove's husband had announced to her that the tribe would be relocating and that preparations would soon be under way for the move.

Red Horse watched the despair on his sister's face and knew his suspicions were right. She had fallen in love with the scout. Then, the decision to move was a wise one for several reasons. Red blood should stay pure or it would bring bad medicine to the tribe. He knew that in time, Prairie Flower would marry one of her own and forget her feelings for the white man. She would grieve for a short time, and then she would be strong.

The beautiful Texas sunset was wasted on Prairie Flower as her heart turned to a stone lump in her chest. She knew that her dreams would not become reality and that her destiny was with her people. She methodically accomplished her evening duties, and an occasional tear would slide down her cheek. Red Horse had been unusually gruff with her today. She could not ever hide her inner self from him and knew that he disapproved of her feelings.

Jeff rose to a sitting position. He had been nursed, once more, back to health. This time he had enjoyed the comfort of his family instead of the coldness of the hospital. Mamie, Samantha, and his nieces had doted on him. He worried about the burden he was to the two women and was glad that the girls were old enough to help. He decided that this time, he would be more patient and not rush himself.

"I can't believe this wonderful fall we've been having. The days have been absolutely gorgeous." Samantha's pleasant voice wafted its way to Jeff's ears. He was thankful his brother had been so blessed with her companionship. The two people on his mind entered the front room at the same time. His brother's countenance told of fresh concerns. Jeff started to question him but decided he would wait until they could be alone.

"Good Afternoon." Gemes tried to sound carefree as he greeted his wife. "Jeff, have you behaved yourself today?" He teased his brother while he hugged Samantha. She knew something was wrong. His cheerfulness was forced, and the muscles in his back were stretched tight beneath his shirt. He could often hide his feelings but not from the two people in his presence. Samantha suspected that relations were unusually tense between the soliers and the current band of Comanche, camped on the banks of Oak Creek.

"I wonder when the first northern will hit. There's not a cloud in the sky right now, but then in West Texas, a person can sure be surprised." Samantha tried to make light conversation to take her husband's mind off of whatever was troubling him. He seldom spent much time in his quarters, because there was always so much work to be done. The past few weeks had been spent fixing damages incurred during the stampede.

Samantha detected that her husband needed to visit with his brother and gracefully excused herself. As she was leaving, Jeff commented, "Big brother, you are one lucky man and don't you ever forget it. Well, maybe Rebecca is a challenge sometimes." He added the last comment with a chuckle, trying to ease some of his brother's tension.

"Jeff, we need to talk. We will be holding another council tomorrow, and I need you by my side. Since we have been having the talks here, getting you to the meeting won't be a problem. I do need your word that you won't try to do a bunch of moving around. I know that the Comanche still make you nervous, but anxiety isn't something you need right now. So, all I'm asking is for you to be a keen observer and give me your perceptions after we are finished. The last thing I can handle is for you to have a relapse. That last setback almost cost you your life." Gemes made one of the longest speeches of his life; he had not ever been one to lecture folks.

"I'm not sure I'm the one anybody needs to be worrying about. You, Captain, have aged ten years in the last two since we have been dealing with the Comanche. First, they send you to Fort Belknap where you had to fight with the Indians almost daily, and the big dogs in Washington griped about that. Then, your orders send you here, you make peace, and they don't like that at all. Now, as for me, all I have to do is sneak around and spy on the Comanche. My job's easy." Jeff did not like attention being called to his weakened condition and did his best to turn the tables.

The truth was that pleasing the politicians in Washington could bring more stress on a man than facing imminent danger. The government never could make up its mind what they really wanted out of the wild frontier. Then, they expected the commanding officers to read their minds.

"At least I don't try to take on rattlesnakes," Gemes retorted and added, "Sometimes I think I'd be more successful than dealing with the politicians. But, now, we have a bigger problem. Red Horse is talking of moving soon. All of our work here may come to naught if he does, because we will become open targets to Yellow Wolf and his gang. The only thing that might save us is if Red Horse's Kiowa friends move closer and provide us with extra protection." Gemes ran his fingers through his hair in a frantic gesture.

"I thought our goal was to get them to reservation land. Is that not what we want?" Jeff asked the captain, puzzled.

"Our goal is to get as many Indians as we can to reservation land with the fewest casualties to our people. Having Red Horse nearby has been accomplishing that end so far. He has a way of convincing the other tribes to cooperate, and he also provides us with added security in the meantime. Besides, he is the first Comanche that I have been able to say I truly trust and it makes me feel a whole lot better to deal with him." Gemes defended his strategy.

"So, why are they suddenly wanting to move. I thought they wanted to avoid the reservation. You have allowed them to stay much longer than anyone else would." Jeff could not comprehend the Comanche's decision.

"I suspect that they have sensed the distrust coming from the fort since the stampede. Look at what has happened across the country. Distrust breeds fear, fear breeds anger, and anger breeds war. Red Horse probably fears we are turning on him, and the safest thing for him to do is leave the area since he has already made an enemy of Yellow Wolf." Gemes explained his speculations.

"Can we convince him otherwise or do you think it is a lost cause?" The scout was beginning to understand the dilemma. Red Horse could not leave or the fort would be left in grave danger.

"That is why I have asked for one more council. Red Horse almost declined, but I promised him another red shirt in trade. Sometimes, I think Mamie's right. There is a little boy in every man that likes a treat every once in awhile." He smiled as he thought about Red Horse's delight in those bright shirts. He reminded his brother again to take life easy and left the house.

The next day, the council was unsuccessful. Red Horse was determined that the majority of the fort believed they were at fault and that nothing but destruction would follow the mishap. He assured the captain that he would speak to the Kiowa and ask for their help on his behalf. He believed that the leader of the white man spoke truths to him, but that his followers would not ever believe a Comanche. No amount of pleading or bartering could change his mind. Jeff sat restlessly on his cot for most of the meeting. Occasionally, he would rise and stand next to the captain. He wanted to pace the floor, but kept his promise to his brother. Gemes felt more despair than he had in a long time.

That night, he retired to his room early without eating any supper. The situation made him feel sick to his stomach. Just a few minutes after he had crawled into bed, there was a knock on the door.

"Gemes, cover yo'self. Yo' Mamie needs to be a talkin' to ya now." She called gently, but firmly through the door. Gemes knew better than to refuse her request, besides, a small part of him longed for her comfort.

"Come on in, Mamie. I'm already in the bed." He tried to sound a little irritated, hoping she would think her mothering annoyed him.

The elderly lady moved to the side of his bed and placed a large, withering hand on his forehead. "Son, you and me, we both be a knowin' I's ain't yo' real momma, but I be raisin' ya fo' a lon' time and I's be a knowin' yo' thoughts most of the time. Now, I done taught ya that the

93

good Lord be goin' afore ya an' fightin' yo' battles. You just leave it all in his han's. Ya hear me now? Now, I's be wantin' ya to git outta that there bed and come fill yo' belly. They ain't a soul alive that be doin' any good without food now." With her mission accomplished she turned to leave the room.

"Mamie wait. I know you're right. Sometimes, when I'm around so much fear and doubt all the time, I forget where we've been and what the good Lord has brought us through. You and I both know that I didn't escape the Comanche on my own. Now, I'm trying to understand them." He grasped his servant's hand, forgetting for a minute that she was not his Ma.

Gemes joined his family at the table after redressing. Rebecca sat quietly at the table, acting unusually calm and quiet. Jeff had been able to eat the last few meals with the family as he was gradually gaining strength. The family bowed their heads to say grace.

"Heavenly Father, we ask today for your strength, guidance, and above all, your will. Sometimes Lord, we may not understand life, but we pray that you will help us face the unknown future, trusting like a child. We ask that you bless the bounty that you have so graciously provided. Amen." The captain ended the prayer and began to eat.

"Pa, I think I'll pray tonight for it to snow tomorrow." Rebecca announced suddenly.

"And just why would you want snow in mid-November Bec?" Her uncle asked her with amusement in his voice.

"Well, if it snows tomorrow, then the Comanche will have to stay and then Pa will have more time to convince them to stay for good. Besides, if it snows, we won't have lessons tomorrow and we can play in it." She announced as if she, personally, had control of the weather. Snow so seldom fell in the area that when it did, Samantha allowed the children a day free of study.

"I be figurin' if we ask anythin' in His name believin' then we be receivin' it." Mamie spoke with certainty from the doorway. She always insisted on serving her family and then eating later despite their protests. Gemes had emphatically told her repeatedly that in Texas, they could do things the way they wanted and not follow the "rules of society." Still, she continuously waited on those she adored.

Samantha cast Eliza a wary look, having noticed earlier in the day that there was not a cloud in the sky. The warm air certainly gave no indication that freezing precipitation was remotely possible. While Samantha had faith, this request was stretching the limits. Gemes looked suspiciously at his daughter wondering how she knew what had been discussed in council. He was raising a child, much more sly than any coyote or Comanche could ever be.

Before going to bed, Rebecca stayed true to her word. She knelt and asked for a snow big enough that the Comanche would not leave and that class would be cancelled. Maybe Little Running Water would even be able to stay long enough to help her find another frog.

Early the next morning, Samantha woke her youngest daughter and told her to go look out the window. There, in white splendor, lay the grounds, covered in at least six inches of snow. Now, there were some that would try to call the incident a chance happening, but Rebecca new it was a miracle. She began to jump up and down and squeal with delight, "I can't believe it; God really did it; He really did just for me."

Suddenly a brilliant idea struck the child, "Ma, can Uncle Jeff help me make a sled and then, can I go slide down that big hill over there?" She thought her plan was grand. Then, her little face fell as her Ma shook her head and began to explain the dangers.

Rebecca decided to enjoy the snow anyway when Ruby told her that someday they would be big enough to slide down any hill they wanted. They decided that the day might even come when the Comanche and the white man lived in perfect harmony and children could roam the area freely. After her miracle, Rebecca decided that someday just might come and bundled herself, ready to play in the snow.

CHAPTER EIGHT

A Thanksgiving Surprise

Just as the snow was starting to melt, another storm came, bringing more freezing weather, sleet, and snow. The Comanche had temporarily delayed their departure. There had been minimal interaction between the two camps since the first freezing precipitation. Little Running Water did manage to sneak close to Rebecca one day when she was outside throwing snowballs at her friends. He wanted to get to know her better and learn more of her language. However, he had been warned to stay clear of the white man until Yellow Wolf's bad medicine disappeared. Red Horse believed that the chief had brought them bad luck and felt the fort was now an imminent threat. He kept the rest of his worries to himself.

As she sat huddled inside her tipi, Prairie Flower was secretly relieved that the bad weather had begun early that year. Maybe, she could learn more about the scout. She had heard that he had survived his setback and was getting stronger. Red Horse had tried to withhold any information from her about the white man, but Little Running Water had managed to spy for her. He was already one of the best trackers in the tribe. She returned her thoughts to the buffalo hide that she was turning into garments for herself and her family members.

On the other side of the creek, Samantha's anxiety grew. With tensions mounting inside the fort, the sight of the tipis brought fear to many. Still, the incident did not make sense to the captain's wife. Why would Red

Horse work so hard for peace and then rush a bunch of buffalo into the fort, causing utter chaos and injuring so many? The hospital had been full since that fateful day. A few had even died. Somehow, this time, she believed Red Horse was innocent. So, what had spooked the beasts? Maybe Yellow Wolf had been at fault. She decided she should call a meeting of the officer's wives and plead the Comanche's case.

Gemes' leadership could only succeed to a point without the support of those under his command. The soldiers readily obeyed him ,but there was a growing restlessness since the disaster. For the first time since he had taken charge at the fort, the captain's wisdom was in question. There were those that used his relationship with his servant as a weapon to undermine his leadership. Gemes was not a man to confront the gossip. Rather, he accomplished his duties with steady determination and acted as if he was in total control.

The children continued playing while the adults struggled with their fear and doubt. Rebecca decided that since Thanksgiving would arrive in a few days that they should reenact the first such holiday. She stood erect and announced, "We have established this colony we call Plymouth on the rocky western shore of Cape Cod Bay in southeastern Massachusetts. We will celebrate a great harvest with our Indian friends."

Ruby burst into laughter at her sister's foolishness. "You are so silly, Bec. I guess you do pay some attention to your lessons after all."

Rebecca did not respond as she had spotted Little Running Water standing behind the dormant Oak tree. He motioned for her to come to him. She looked at her sister and sadly shook her head. She knew Ruby often covered for her, but that playing with a Comanche was stretching the boundaries of her sister's tolerance. Little Running Water understood the reason for his friend's rejection but it still hurt. He would come again when she was alone.

Later that evening, Samantha payed a visit to Arizona's hut. She wanted her help in bringing some sense of stability back to the fort. She had shared her ideas with her husband earlier in the day, and he had seemed eager to let her shoulder some of his burden. His only request had been that she allow him to accompany her; he did not want her falling, as the baby was due in less than six weeks. They were eagerly anticipating their Christmas bundle.

"Mrs. Blair. Captain." One of the soldiers spoke to her and saluted her husband, but she heard a hint of resentment in his voice. She wondered how quickly word would reach Washington about the disaster and the blame placed on her husband. Many of his subordinates felt him entirely at fault for ever trusting Red Horse. As she walked hand in hand with Gemes, Samantha felt a peace come over her, reassuring her that everything was going to be fine.

Lieutenant Samuel Cain had been assigned to the post under the leadership of Captain Gemes Blair, and the two had quickly developed a special kind of trust. When Gemes was faced with difficult decisions, his first lieutenant backed him. Although the two men did not always see eye to eye on every issue, Samuel had quickly learned that his captain did not make plans in haste. Rather, he contemplated his moves carefully and weighed all possible outcomes before acting. Therefore, Samuel felt comfortable giving his unconditional support. Arizona and Samantha's friendship also brought them together in times of trouble.

"I saw Jeff sitting on the porch today. I'm glad to see he's gaining his strength. Do you figure on keeping him still for long? I sure would hate to see him go back to scouting before spring." Samuel stood outside the hut talking to the captain while the two women were inside the meager shelter.

"I suspect if he even takes a notion of walking ten yards without help, Mamie and Samantha will have him hog-tied." Gemes also knew that his little brother's last scare had gotten his attention, at least for the time being.

"What are our wives discussing in there? I know that the two of you did not walk all the way over here in this weather just to chat, especially not with her being in the family way and all." Samuel had a feeling that Gemes' very sage wife had found a possible solution to their problems.

"Come to the front of my quarters at nine tomorrow morning and you will see. I have been sworn to secrecy." Gemes kept very little from his faithful assistant, but this time he was playing the cards Samantha's way.

Samuel cast the captain a questioning look and before he had time to press the issue, the two women walked outside. The couples said their farewells, and the captain and his wife made the cold trek back to their rock house.

Arizona whistled a tune as she placed the meal on the table. Her heart beat a happy rhythm in her chest. She felt more at peace than she had in days, and her spirit was contagious. Her husband was not sure what Samantha had said to uplift his wife, but the hope of something better provided him with a good night's sleep.

With the sun glistening on the white wonderland, the small group of women made their way to the front of the commanding officer's quarters. Icicles hung in various shapes and sizes from the eaves of the rock house. The cold wind nipped at any exposed flesh and the ladies huddled as close as possible to each other. Samantha stepped to the front of the porch with her husband, Jeff, and Samuel standing behind her for support. Rebecca and Ruby had been awakened early that morning and asked to deliver the invitations. They were as anxious as everyone else to learn what their mother had to say. She was usually a reserved woman who was content to let her husband stand in the limelight. Today, she had taken the lead.

"Good morning ladies. I will try to keep what I have to say brief. I do ask that you hear me out before you turn a deaf ear. I have been much like all of you with our fears, doubts, frustrations, and blame. However, I have done a great deal of thinking and praying and feel that we need to reexamine our thoughts and actions. On December 13, 1621, the Indians and the Pilgrims came together for three days of feasting, prayer, and thanksgiving. I realize that we have not enjoyed the bounty of the harvest the pilgrims did that year, but we have all been spared our lives from a terrible tragedy. While I understand the devastation and loss of lives that we have suffered, I also realize that we are still alive. The tragedy could have been so much worse. At first I was like all of you. I thought that Red Horse was to blame, but he denies any involvement. For some reason, I believe him. Just suppose for one moment that Yellow Wolf staged this entire incident just to get us at odds with Red Horse. You see, he knows if Red Horse leaves then this fort will be left vulnerable to his attacks." Samantha paused and waited for her ideas to take root in their minds.

She continued after a few moments of silence, "Now, I have a plan. I know that feeding the entire tribe is out of the question. We do not have that much food available. However, we can feed the leaders and their wives. We must convince Red Horse that we believe him and do not blame him for what has happened. Think about it ladies! Why would he bring destruction to his own camp just to hurt us? It doesn't make any sense. Yellow Wolf had to be behind all of this and we must not be left at his mercy. So, what do you say? Let's fix a big Thanksgiving Day feast and invite the leaders of the tribe and their families to celebrate with us. I cannot think of a better time to offer them our blessings and peace." She ended her speech breathing a silent prayer to herself.

At first the group of ladies stood in speechless awe of the captain's wife. Then, murmurs were heard among the group. Samantha grew restless as she watched them whispering among themselves. Then from the back of the crowd Arizona spoke, "I will bring a custard pie. I think Mrs. Blair has the right idea."

One by one, Arizona's offer was followed by others as the women of Fort Chadbourne bound their hearts and minds together. They decided on dishes they could make from their meager supplies. Hope had once more returned to the fort. A meek, determined soldier had made the difference, and she did not have to wear a uniform to accomplish her victory.

The next day, Gemes and Samuel rode to the Comanche camp and extended the invitation. Red Horse snorted in protest. Gemes stood puzzled. He thought that the whole problem had been that the chief felt unwelcome in the area. So, why the rejection of peace? Maybe, he thought they were trying to trick him. As Gemes stood thinking of his next course of action, one of the elders of the tribe motioned for Red Horse. The two officers stood nervously waiting his return.

Red Horse and the tribal elder had their backs to the two soldiers, but there was obviously a disagreement taking place. The captain suspected that the elder did not approve of Red Horse's objections. Gemes did not understand the uncharacteristic behavior himself. He tried to speculate about possible reasons for Red Horse's actions and could think of none.

Meanwhile, the council chief had himself a big problem. With the white man offering peace, how could he justify the continued hostilities? Yet, if the tribe learned of his connection to the chief, then he would lose the respect of his clan and be ousted from his position. Maybe, he could use the captain's strong medicine as an excuse for his weakness. No, he must not appear feeble for any reason. For now, there was nothing for him to do except go along with the planned feast and hope that his secret would stay hidden.

The two natives returned to the soldiers with a decision made. They would celebrate Thanksgiving together and renew the peace between them. Gemes and Samuel mounted their horses and returned to the fort, leaving behind an extremely troubled Comanche chief.

The cool, crisp dawn announced the arrival of Thanksgiving Day. The sun made its appearance, but the temperatures prevented most of the snow from melting. Despite the cold, the officer's wives rose early, bustling to prepare the noonday meal. In the captain's kitchen, Eliza was dipping a rooster in a pot of boiling water while Ruby sliced some bread and filled a bowl with jam. The two worked in silence knowing that when Rebecca joined them there would be plenty of chatter.

As she trudged through the snow carrying the milk bucket her uncle had handed her, Rebecca looked furtively around her, hoping to catch a glimpse of Little Running Water. Since his father was the chief, surely he would be invited to the festivities. The soldiers had agreed, somewhat reluctantly to move their cots to the sides of the barracks. Then, a makeshift table had been fixed of roughhewn logs. The long building was the only place that would hold everyone for the meal.

The kitchen door opened, and Rebecca handed the pail to her Mamie. She tried not to show her excitement at the prospect of getting to finally eat with the Comanche. However, Eliza knew her little girl's heart and was secretly sharing her delight. She looked out the window and saw their visitors making their way into the camp.

Gemes noticed, as he made his way to the kitchen to offer his assistance, that there were no horses in sight. Trust did not come easy for the soldiers, and they feared their mounts would be stolen. He chuckled to himself, knowing that no white man could hide much from the Comanche. If they took a notion to find and steal the horses, they would.

The captain had put his wife to bed that morning, suspecting that the baby was coming early. He needed to let Mamie know and take her place in the kitchen. He did not know much about cooking, but felt much more comfortable there, versus delivering a child. He would trust Mamie to tend to his wife and baby.

Samantha lay on her bed, staring at the ceiling. She hated to be leaving Mamie with all of the preparations for the day, but she knew that the baby would be making an early arrival sometime that day. She tried not to worry, concerned about her new addition being born too soon. She was excited that the women had responded so well to her ideas and had been able to persuade their husbands to cooperate.

The door to her room opened and Eliza entered with supplies in her hands. She informed Samantha that she had already sent for the doctor, and he should be arriving shortly. She also relayed the information that the natives were beginning to gather near the barracks. As she watched Mamie bustle about the room, making delivery preparations, she suddenly felt a peace surround her.

The captain tried hard to make a pretense of enjoying himself throughout the meal. Red Horse had arrived with his four wives. Native customs allowed the common Comanche only one wife, subordinate officers two wives, the war chief three, and the civil chief four. Since the women did most of the work, having more that one wife was a status symbol to the Comanche. The men planned wars, hunted, and slept while the women tended to their every need.

Prairie Flower had been allowed to attend but was cautioned to keep a low profile. She and Jeff tried hard not to watch each other, but as the day progressed their efforts became futile. She also knew that she would receive a tongue lashing from her brother when they returned to camp, but she did not care.

Meanwhile in the commanding officer's quarters, Eliza was assisting Doctor Denson with a delivery. A strapping, little boy, Joseph Curtis Blair, made his entrance into the world. While mother and son rested, the doctor went in search of the captain to share the good news.

Cheers rose inside the barracks as the captain had announced the new arrival. Although his son was early, he still weighed an estimated seven pounds. Doctor Denson rarely missed a baby's weight by more than a few ounces. Delivering a healthy child was one of the few bright spots in his career. Those rare moments of delight kept him from losing his mind over all the deaths he could not prevent.

After welcoming his son to the world and checking on his wife, Gemes joined his brother on the porch. The day had provided some sense of ease, but there was still a bit of an underlying current between the soldiers and the Comanche. Trust did not come easy for either side and once broken, was difficult to regain. The captain was glad to, at last, be in comfortable companionship with Jeff.

"Well, big brother, looks like you finally got yourself a namesake." Jeff tried to sound casual, but he was as excited about the new arrival as anyone.

"I reckon I do. Not that I'll think anymore of him than I do my girls though." Gemes responded with a big grin. He missed the time he used to spend with his children, teaching them how to make things and sometimes, just having fun with them.

"Today gave us several things to be thankful for didn't it?" Jeff walked to the front of the porch and lit his pipe. He knew that his brother was likely to start quizzing him about Red Horse's sister, and he did not want to have to look him in the eye.

"Yeah, like a chance to get a closer look at a certain Comanche woman." The captain chuckled, poking fun at the scout. He was one of the few inhabitants of the fort that would not fault his brother for falling in love with a Comanche, especially not one that had saved his life.

"Now, we aren't going to discuss that topic, so, you just might as well drop it. I done told you that I'll get married the day a woman loves me as much as Bec does, and that's not likely to happen." He took a puff of the tobacco and slowly exhaled the smoke.

"Someday, Jefferson Davis Blair, a female's going to come along that will have you eating out of her hand. You just wait and see." Gemes punched him in the arm and started into the house.

"Yeah, someday, maybe." Jeff followed his brother, glad for the conversation to be ended. He seriously doubted that someday would ever come.

CHAPTER NINE

SOMEDAY

December brought continuing cold temperatures, but not much precipitation. Occasionally, snow flurries would drift through the air, painting a winter scene across the vast Texas sky. There were no usual festivities being planned and no Christmas decorations adorning the buildings. The soldiers continued with their duties while the few women and children in the camp longed for family and friends. Red Horse had resigned himself to the fact that his tribe would not be able to relocate until spring. Samantha held school as often as the temperatures and circumstances permitted.

One morning, the sun broke through the dreariness, lighting the sky with its presence. Samantha bounced down the front steps as soon as the breakfast dishes were done. She spotted her Ma leaning over a washtub and ran to peer at her baby brother. Curtis had inherited a head full of curly locks from Samantha's side of the family. His hair was jet black like his mother's too. The one trait that made Rebecca especially proud was his green eyes, just like hers and her Pa's. Ma said most babies eyes were blue, but Curtis' eyes were already very defined emeralds.

"Ma, do you want me to take Curtis with me to play? I'll watch him good." Rebecca was thrilled to finally be the big sister for a change. She did not understand why she could not play with the infant like a doll. Toys were few in the fort. Besides, a real baby was much more fun than a pretend one.

"That is very kind of you to offer. I know you would watch him closely, but the air is a bit cool still. I think when I finish here, I should probably take him in the house with me." Samantha declined her offer gently. She did not have the courage to tell her daughter that a one-month old baby was not ready to play.

Jeff watched the scene from his brother's porch. He was becoming increasingly anxious to get back on the trail. His leg was healing, but he still walked with a limp. He suspected that the injury must have damaged the muscles in his calf. He just knew that if he got back to work the muscles would heal themselves. He thought about riding to the Indian camp and asking for some more snakeweed. Maybe it would help him continue to mend.

"Hi, Uncle Jeff. Whatcha doin'?" Rebecca flopped down beside her favorite person and laid her head on his shoulder.

Jeff placed his arm around his nieces tiny shoulders and gave her a squeeze. "Hello, Bec. I don't know about you, but I kind of think it's nice to see the sun shining."

"Yes sir it is. Maybe, you and I can find me another frog today. Little Running Water accidentally let mine go and he went up Ma's skirts and then ran away. Oh, yeah, and I promised not to bring any more critters in the house, EVER!" She let her confession escape her lips before she realized how badly she was incriminating herself.

Jeff could not keep from laughing. The sound started in his belly and rolled out in one fluid motion. He delighted in the stunned look on his niece's face; she could not believe she had just told on herself.

"A promise is a promise Bec. You know that," Jeff tried to say sternly after regaining his composure.

"I know." Rebecca placed her chin in the palms of her hands, looking dejected. She had just admitted that the mischievous frog had been hers, and now, the truth was known. "You won't tell Ma will you Uncle Jeff. If you won't I will keep my promise?" Rebecca made an attempt at bribery.

"But, you didn't promise that you wouldn't catch any. You just promised not to take them in the house right." Jeff felt mildly guilty about encouraging his niece to explore and providing her with a loophole to her promise.

The sentence had barely left his lips before Jeff was receiving a big kiss on his forehead from his niece. Then, she sprinted across the dead grass in search of a new pet. She was so excited that she forgot that frogs did not do much hopping around in the winter. In the spring and summer, they were all over the place, but when it was cold, they were nowhere to be found. She realized her search was in vain and headed back to her house. Suddenly, she heard a strange sound coming from behind an Oak tree. She paused, cautiously, for a minute, and then, her curiosity got the best of her.

The little brown hand had covered her mouth before she had time to squeal in delight. Little Running Water was beaming. He could finally share his new word with his pal. He had been waiting for days for the opportunity to present itself.

"Little Running Water learn new word." He then pointed to Rebecca and then to himself and said, "Friends, Little Running Water and white girl, friends." He proclaimed his discovery proudly.

"Yes, Little Running Water, you are my friend and I am very proud of you for learning new words. Now, you will have to teach me more Comanche." While the boy did not understand much of what Rebecca said, he did perceive that she was proud of him.

The two stood, hidden, in the tall grasses, making gestures to each other. Rebecca would use sign language and then, say words in English. She burst into laughter at Little Running Water's attempt to say frog. His thick Comanche tongue made the word difficult for him to pronounce.

"Rebecca Jane Blair, where are you? You know that you give me a fright when you run off like this." Rebecca heard her mother calling and ran to the house with a happy heart.

Rebecca stirred the pot of stew and hummed to herself. The mixture consisted of deer meat and rice. The few cans of vegetables from Mamie's meager garden were quickly dwindling and thus, being saved for Christmas dinner. Samantha walked into the kitchen and smiled at her daughter. She enjoyed her children and loved to see them content.

"Ma, since you invited the Indians to Thanksgiving, can, I mean, may I invite them to Christmas." Rebecca just knew that this time, her mother would be in agreement with her plans.

"Now, Rebecca, you know that I still do not feel safe with you out of my sight. You must remember that the Comanche are still savages. They cannot totally be trusted. I was merely offering some sort of compromise to ease the situation. Anyway, I am planning to have our Christmas dinner in our quarters with our family and close friends. In the afternoon, I will open our front room to the soldiers for coffee and cake. As you know, most of them are here without their families." Samantha left the kitchen house and signaled the end to the conversation. Rebecca knew that it was pointless to argue.

Eliza watched her lovely lady crossing the yard from the kitchen to the house. Her long skirt swirling around her ankles. Her bonnet was starched, crisp, as usual. She suspected that Rebecca had, once more, tried her patience. Her mouth was set in a stern line that signaled a solemn mood.

The Blair family met in the dining room, as usual, for supper. Everyone was present, except Rebecca. Gemes and Samantha looked at each other with concern in their eyes. Eliza had told them to go ahead with the meal, and she would go see if she could find her.

The blessing was said over the food, and the eating began in silence. Ruby knew that her sister was impulsive and high-spirited and surmised that she was still pouting in the kitchen. Suddenly, the front door swung open, and Eliza rushed into the room, in a frenzy.

"Mistuh Gemes, I's can' be findin' our baby anywhere. She must've let that bad tempa' of hers be gittin' the best of her. We hafta go a lookin' fo' the chil'!" Her fear was evident in her voice and her face, and she typically was not one to panic.

Chairs were shoved back from the table as everyone rushed into action. Jeff was the first one out the door, with his older brother close behind him. As they were coming down the steps, Red Horse rode into the yard to meet them.

"Red Horse look for Little Running Water. He no come to tipi for eat!" The civil chief conveyed his message in broken English. Apparently, there were two children missing. Gemes noticed that the Comanche wore only leggings and no shirt. He appeared to have been lazing around his camp when he realized his son was missing. He, too, must have discovered the children's friendship.

"Red Horse, Rebecca, my daughter, is missing too. They must have run away together. We will organize a search party and..." Gemes voice trailed to a stop as realization finally hit him full force in the face. He was staring into the same eyes that had held sympathy for him; Red Horse had untied him from that stump.

The captain stood in stunned silence as he suddenly understood what had been happening since the stampede. At some point during that time, Red Horse had realized the connection and been afraid that his moment of weakness would be discovered by his tribe. Now, the captain knew the real reason the chief was trying to break the bond between them. He must convince Red Horse that their secret would remain between them forever. For now, however, there were two missing youngsters that needed to be found.

Red Horse watched the light of realization dawn in those piercing, green eyes. He had stayed too long. Now, there would be nothing for him to do but hope for the captain's continued loyalty. The spirits were bringing his punishment on him, but had they not driven him to the action he had taken? He did not understand his spirit world sometimes. Right now, he must focus and bring

116

the captain's daughter safely home, or he would face a wrath worse than the spirit world could render.

"Red Horse think Little Running Water track girl. He best tracker of Comanche." The boy had already risen in status among the youth of the tribe for his superior tracking and hunting skills. He also had his father's way with the people.

"Can you track Little Running Water?" Gemes asked the question and then added, "Of course, you can. He learned from the best." He voiced his confidence in the chief. Gemes and Jeff mounted their horses and followed Red Horse out of the fort.

Eliza did her best to comfort the fearful, grieving mother. Samantha sat on a chair in the front room. The warm fireplace did not stop the chill in her bones. Mamie entered the main house with a cup of coffee and placed it on the table in front of her lady. Samantha's jet, black hair was fixed in a tidy twist as usual, but her soul felt anything but in control. She knew her fear and distrust were to blame for her child's behavior. She must let go of all her anger and allow herself to heal, or she would not ever know complete peace.

Meanwhile, somewhere north of the fort, Little Running Water carefully tracked his friend. Why would she leave the safety of her camp? Did she not know that Yellow Wolf could be near and capture her? He must find her before any renegades did. They would capture her, torture her, and possibly, kill her.

Rebecca finally stopped running and flopped down underneath a tree to rest. She was so mad at her Ma. Why could she not have a Comanche friend? Mamie was not white; why was red skin any different? She did not understand her Ma's way of thinking.

A small, brown hand closed on Rebecca's shoulder, and she knew Little Running Water had tracked her. The two sat in silence for a long time. Little Running Water did not know what troubled his little friend, but he knew he must keep her safe. He would not let any harm come to her.

Several hours passed, and the two women continued to pace and pray. Ruby would join them every few minutes, hoping any second the door would open and her sister would be safe in the house. She knew that there were many dangers in the vast land, which could take her sister from them forever. Oh, why did Rebecca have to be so impulsive?

Ruby's thoughts were interrupted as the front door slowly swung open. Jeff entered the room, limping on his slowly, improving leg. He looked much older than his twenty-two years. The fear of losing his niece, coupled with the stress of the last few months, had aged him considerably. The harsh life of the frontier tended to hasten the aging process for many. He crossed to the table and hung his hat on the back of the chair before saying a word.

"Gemes and Rebecca are in the kitchen, talking. I didn't figure what they had to say was any of my business. So, I came on in to let you ladies know that we had found her. Actually, that little Comanche boy had tracked her and Red Horse tracked him. We spotted them about three miles north of here. How those two managed to make it that far that fast is beyond me." He gingerly lowered his sore frame into the chair and accepted the cup of coffee that Mamie was offering him. Samantha began to weep and release all of her pent-up tension.

While the captain, the scout, and the chief were searching, a group of Comanche had gathered just outside the fort. Jeff had passed them on his way to the house. He had glanced briefly in the direction of Prairie Flower and then quickly averted his eyes from her. She wondered if, someday, he might try to get to know her better. She knew his job was to travel, and that someday might be a long time in coming. She decided she could wait.

Red Horse motioned for the members of his tribe to take Little Running Water back to camp. He was proud of his son. His superior tracking skills had most likely just saved the little, white girl's life. Now, the time had come for him to plead his case with the captain. He waited until the Comanche party were out of sight before he turned his horse toward the officer's quarters.

Gemes stood on the porch. Jeff had not joined him, as he usually did; he felt there was something his older brother needed to face on his own. He was unsure of what was troubling the captain, but he knew it went far beyond Rebecca's outburst. The captain stared into the black night and heard a horse approaching his quarters.

The Comanche dismounted and tied his horse to the post. He slowly made his way up the steps, lighting his peace pipe on the way. He extended the pipe to Gemes in an offering of peace. Although the captain hated smoking, he usually accepted the offer during peace talks, out of a feeling of obligation. He choked on the puff of smoke that hit his lungs, and he could not prevent himself from coughing. He thought he detected a slight smile trying to escape Red Horse's stern expression.

"Red Horse, my friend, it seems I owe you a great deal. First, you save my life and now, your son has saved my daughter's." He looked at the chief with a new admiration. He must convince his Comanche counterpart that their secret would forever be only theirs to share with fondness.

"Red Horse no weak." He spat on the ground for emphasis. "The spirits, they make me let white boy loose. The tribe no think Red Horse weak man. Red Horse no want to set boy free. The spirits drive me." He pleaded his case with the captain.

A few seconds of silence followed as the captain thought of the right words to reassure the chief. He finally decided one word was all that was needed. The stars sparkled in agreement.

"My friend, your secret is safe with me, but come, it's time you learned a new word." Captain Gemes Blair turned his eyes to the clouds and uttered a single sound, "Angels."